Other Titles by Jill Myles

The Snow Queen's Captive

By Jill Myles

Chapter One

This was like a bad acid trip.

Or at least it would be, Charlotte decided, if she'd ever tried acid. Had to be too much laughing gas. Had to be. Why else would she be blinking up at the sight of a little old woman with a smiling, wrinkled face, a halo of white cherub curls, and a party hat on her head? Charlotte blinked her eyes slowly, glancing over to her right. On her other side loomed a woman with a youthful round face, pink eyebrows, and tufts of hair that looked like cotton candy. She held a unicorn horn in her hand and her skin sparkled in the clinical light of the dentist's office.

Charlotte closed her eyes and counted to five, hoping the vision would go away. She was really going to have to talk to Dr. Franks about how much laughing gas he was giving her. The fact that she was seeing things that seemed straight out of a psychedelic kids' TV show come to life?

Told her that whatever she was on, the dosage was a wee bit too high. At least her mouth didn't hurt. Her tooth had been throbbing for days before she'd finally conquered her fear of a root canal and decided to head in to the dentist. She'd been so shaky with fear that he'd suggested nitrous. And even though she'd never had nitrous before, she'd gone along with it.

No one had told her it'd make her hallucinate, though.

Fingers tapped her cheek. "Wake up, sweetie pie. Rise and shine."

Could hallucinations be tactile?

Something hard poked her nose. "BOOP."

An exasperated sigh echoed in her ear. "Not right now, Fifi. This is a sensitive part of the process. She's going to be disoriented, so we need to be sensitive to her needs. That's fairy godmother one-oh-one. You certainly don't 'boop' a client on the nose when they first come to."

"But her nose is just so cute!" The lighter voice sounded miffed.

"No booping the clients! Write that down."

Charlotte's eyes fluttered open and she glanced around. Still the older woman and the young cotton-candy one, though the latter was now scribbling with a purple feather pen into a Lisa Frank notepad. "No booping," Cotton-Candy said to herself as she wrote. "Got it."

"Look, she's waking up." The elderly woman smiled down at Charlotte. "Now smile and look friendly."

Cotton-Candy bared her teeth in a frozen, too-wide grin, looking more like a jack-o-lantern than a friend.

Charlotte smacked her lips, and then frowned. "Who are you guys?" Her hand went to her lip, which was no longer numb. Weird. She didn't even have any dental equipment in her mouth anymore. Her head was muzzy, too. Had too much time passed? "Did I fall asleep?"

"No, you died," Cotton-Candy said helpfully.

"I *what?*"

The elderly woman reached over and smacked Cotton-Candy on the shoulder. "Sensitivity, Fifi! Sensitivity!"

2

"Sorry." Cotton-Candy blinked rapidly and looked as if she were ready to cry. "I was just trying to help."

Another sigh. "I know. But just let me handle things. You just observe, understand me? Observe." The elderly woman enunciated the word 'observe'. "Can you do that?"

Cotton-Candy nodded.

"I think I'm having a bad nitrous trip," Charlotte whispered, her gaze moving back and forth between the two women.

"That's why we're here to talk to you, my dear," the elderly woman said in a kind voice. She reached out and patted Charlotte's cheek. "Why don't you sit up so we can talk?"

Charlotte did, giving Cotton-Candy a wary look. The pink-haired girl was watching her with an almost hungry look in her gaze, and it was more than slightly unnerving. Despite the weirdness of her situation, though, she felt fine. Now that she was awake, her head was clearing. The constant ache that had been in her jaw for the last week or so was gone. She touched her cheek, surprised to find it was no longer swollen, either. "Wow, that dentist works fast."

"Yes, about that," the elderly woman said. She adjusted her party hat, tilting it so it hung on her head at a rakish angle. "The dentist doesn't actually work that fast. He actually hasn't started working on you at all."

Charlotte frowned, touching her jaw again. "But I feel better."

"I know you do. Allow me to explain." Her hands went to her chest and she beamed at Charlotte. "My name is Muffin, and I'm your fairy godmother."

Charlotte stared at the woman. Fairy...godmother? A purple feather danced into view at the corner of her eye, and she looked over to see Cotton-Candy hastily scribbling notes. She glanced back at the elderly woman - Muffin. "Um, what?"

"I'm your fairy godmother, here to guide you through this difficult time." Her small, soft hands took Charlotte's and she patted it. "Now listen very carefully, my dear, and above all else, I want you to relax and not panic, all right? We're here to take care of things."

"Take...care...things..." Cotton-Candy muttered as she wrote furiously.

Charlotte gave her a wary look, and then turned back to Muffin. "Who's she?"

"That's Fifi, my intern." The smile on her face turned a little more pained. "Work exchange program."

"What do you mean, fairy godmother?" Charlotte rubbed her cheek again. This was all so weird.

Muffin's face wreathed into a sympathetic smile. "Did you know that you were allergic to nitrous, my dear?"

"I am?"

"You are."

"Is that why I'm having all these weird dreams?"

Those little hands kept patting hers. "You did have an adverse reaction, but it's not quite as simple to explain as dreams."

"You died," Fifi blurted again, earning herself another head-shake from Muffin.

"There's good news and bad news," Muffin said. "Which part do you want first?"

"Um, the bad news?" Charlotte asked, wincing a little at the thought.

"The bad news is that you died," Muffin said, nodding. "Fifi's right. You had an allergic reaction to the nitrous and your throat closed up. You died before the dentist realized the problem."

Charlotte gaped at her for a moment longer, and then shook her head. This was too weird. Had to be a laughing gas reaction. "So what's the good news, then?"

Muffin beamed at her, and the hands gave hers a squeeze. "The good news is that your fairy godmother is here and I'm going to give you another shot at life! You'll be given a task that you must complete. If you do so, you win a second go-around. If you lose, well, you've already had all the bad news."

Charlotte pulled her hand from Muffin's clinging grip. "And you're sure this is not a reaction to the laughing gas? Because this definitely seems...trippy."

"She doesn't believe you," Fifi said, her tone almost gleeful with excitement. "Can we show her? Please? Can we show her?"

Muffin gave a gusty sigh and got to her feet, dusting off her white party dress, complete with ruffled crinolines. "All right. I guess we should."

"Show me what?" Charlotte watched the two women get to their feet, her brow furrowing. "What are you going to show me?"

Muffin opened the door to the small dental office and gestured for Charlotte to follow her. "The truth."

As soon as they stepped out of the small office that Charlotte had been resting in, they plunged into chaos. People were everywhere — paramedics, police officers, weeping dental assistants. Nearby, Dr. Franks was talking to a police officer, his thin hair disheveled. His eyes were red, as if he'd been crying. Behind the mob of people, lights flashed from the ambulance parked just outside the windows.

This was confusing. What had happened? As Charlotte watched, the team of paramedics headed toward one part of the room, and her gaze was drawn to the dentist's chair. A white sheet had been tossed over the entire thing, but there was no mistaking the lumps underneath the sheet - a body.

And when they lifted the body out of the chair, a hand fell free, and there was no mistaking that pink

5

gemstone bracelet. It perfectly matched her blingy pink sandals that she'd worn this morning. Charlotte glanced down at her feet, but the shoes were still on there.

For that matter, she was still here, with the two strange women at her side, and no one seemed to be paying the slightest bit of attention to them. Charlotte glanced around at the scene, and then turned to Muffin. "I'm....really confused."

Muffin nodded. "Happens to everyone, my dear."

"Everyone...confused..." Fifi wrote furiously, not looking up from her notebook.

Muffin cast her an exasperated look and moved forward to put an arm around Charlotte's waist. She carefully turned her around and steered her back to the private room they'd emerged from. "No need to see more of this, my dear. Come with me and we'll figure things out, all right? I have plenty to explain."

Charlotte nodded, allowing the woman to gently push her back into the room. Her brain wasn't processing what she just saw. It just wasn't. It...looked like she was dead. But how could that be? She was right here?

But everyone was ignoring her...

Muffin sat Charlotte down in a chair - used for teeth cleaning, Charlotte idly noticed - and took a seat next to her. Fifi sat on one of the counters at the back of the room, watching them and still taking notes. "Now," Muffin said carefully. "There's been a small problem—"

"Problem?" Charlotte's voice rose a hysterical note, all of this finally getting to her. She gestured at the other room, still swarming with people. "Did you see all that out there? Why—"

"Shhh," Muffin said. "Let's calm down and I'll explain." Her voice took on a soothing tone. "There was an accident. No one could have predicted this sort of thing. It's unfortunate, but what's even more unfortunate is that you are one of the few people that have been knocked out of the weave."

"The...weave?"

"The weave of souls. It's all very complicated and probably shouldn't be explained while your brain is mush." Muffin reached over and patted her hand. "What it means is that you have an unfulfilled destiny, my girl. And fairy godmothers like myself, and uh, someday, Miss Fifi over there," her voice got a little strained at the thought, though the smile remained, "are here to help you transition over."

"Transition? To...Heaven?" Charlotte wrapped her arms around herself, hugging. "I don't think I'm ready to go. There are still so many things I wanted to do. I—"

"I know," Muffin said, interrupting. "But you're actually not going anywhere. Like I said, you fell out of the weave."

"Fell....out...of...weave," Fifi intoned as she scribbled notes.

Charlotte blinked. Tried to process this. Failed. "Okay, I give up. I don't understand."

"You can't go anywhere or else it would have already happened."

"Okay, now I *really* don't understand."

"You don't exist anymore, period. Your soul is in limbo. That's why I'm here." And she gave Charlotte a beaming smile to take away the terror from her words. "My job is to make you earn a second chance at life. I can put you in a new scenario and give you a task. If you prove yourself worthy and complete the task in the timeframe allotted, you win a second chance at life and a new beginning."

"A new beginning? As in...like a baby? Reincarnation?"

"Oooo," Fifi cooed, entranced by this idea. "Can we do that? Can we make her a turtle? I love turtles."

"We're not making anyone a turtle," Muffin said in a strained voice. She focused on Charlotte, ignoring her intern. "If you win your second chance, you start fresh in a new place and time. I have to put you in to patch a weak spot in the weave to prevent other people from slipping through the cracks. But since I'm not in charge of the weave, I don't know the place or time that you'd be sent to, only that it's a second chance. Sound good?"

"Not really?" Charlotte began to shiver, rubbing her arms. "Can't I go back to being me? I like my life." It wasn't the most fun or glamorous life in the world, but it was nice and safe. She had a decent job working at a craft store, was going to school at night to finish her college degree in business, and had her own apartment. If there wasn't a boyfriend or lover in her life, it was simply because she didn't have time and she told herself that those things would come later.

Except now? It sounded like 'later' was never going to get here. And that made her cold all over.

Muffin shook her head, fluttering the colored tassels on her party hat. "I'm afraid not."

"But you said if I won, I could patch the weave so other people can't fall through." Heck, saying that aloud, she still wasn't sure this wasn't some sort of bad nitrous trip. "Can't I patch my own weave?"

"You cannot. You don't have a body to return to. Yours is dead."

She couldn't help but flinch at that. Dead was so very...final. "What happens if I fail?"

Muffin spread her hands. "Then I can't help you. You remain outside of the weave forever."

Charlotte's eyes widened and her stomach gave a sick clench. "Um, that doesn't sound good."

"No, it doesn't." Muffin gave her a bright smile and leaned in to pat her knee. "So don't fail, okeydokey?"

"O-okay." She was starting to get more than a little scared. What happened if she remained here out of the weave — or whatever it was — forever? Would she exist without anyone able to see her? Ever? That sounded...disturbing. "So what do I do? What's my task? When do I start?"

Charlotte crossed her fingers, praying that it'd be easy and fool-proof.

"You'll start right away," Muffin said, pulling out a tiny pink handbag and opening it. "We've found that you have the best chance of not getting all messed up in the head from the whole death thing—" she waved a hand in the air as if dying was no big deal, "—if you have a new focus right away. And since I'm a fairy godmother, we deal with fairy tales."

"Fairy tales? Like...the Little Mermaid?"

"Not that one," Muffin said, reaching into her bag and pulling out a tiny, fat book the size of a matchbook. She tapped the cover twice and the book expanded from matchbook-size to encyclopedia-size, covering the fairy godmother's lap. Charlotte's eyes widened in surprise at the sight, but neither Fifi nor Muffin blinked an eye at this remarkable growth. Instead, Muffin opened the book and began to flip through pages. "I've already got someone running her paces through the Mermaid test. I've picked something else for you."

"Oh. Okay." Charlotte leaned forward, watching over Muffin's lap as the fairy godmother picked through dog-eared pages, seemingly searching for something.

After a moment, Muffin patted a page with satisfaction. "Ah! Here we go. The Snow Queen."

Charlotte thought for a moment, and then shook her head. "I don't know that one. What do I have to do?"

"You don't know the Snow Queen?" Muffin looked at her in surprise, and then shook her head. "Kids these days. Fifi, do you know the Snow Queen tale?"

Fifi thought for a moment, then shook her head, her cotton-candy pink hair flying. "Nope!"

Muffin sighed and gave Charlotte a chagrined look. "So hard to find good help these days." She smoothed a hand down her rustling pale skirts. "All right. I'm not much of a storyteller, but I can give you a nice recap at least. The Snow Queen fairy tale is about a young woman who is in love with her childhood sweetheart, a nice young hunk of man-meat. One day he's stolen away by the snow queen, and the enterprising young woman must go and steal him back before he's completely surrendered to the snow queen. There are a few variations on the tale, but if you don't rescue him, the Snow Queen conquers the entire kingdom and blankets it in frost forever."

"No pressure," Charlotte said wryly. "Just the fate of an entire kingdom and a perfect stranger on my shoulders, right?"

"As well as that of your own fate," Muffin agreed. "But yes, more or less. Are you up to it?"

"Do I have a choice?"

"Oh, sweetie," Muffin reached forward and patted her knee. "Do we ever have a choice about when we die?"

Good point. At least she was getting a second chance. Charlotte pressed her hands to her forehead, trying to memorize the task. "Okay. Save guy from snow queen and save the world. Got it. Is there a time limit?"

"One month."

That didn't feel like enough time, but Charlotte supposed she didn't have much of a position to bargain from. "All right, I'll see what I can do."

"Try not to confront the queen directly, as she's very powerful," Muffin told her.

That was a little scary. "You do realize that I'm a fabric salesgirl at a craft shop? I'm not exactly Genghis Khan or Luke Skywalker here."

10

"You do realize nothing requires me to give you a second chance?" Muffin said in a sweet voice laced with steel.

"Good point," Charlotte said. "When do we get started?"

Muffin waved a hand at Fifi, instructing her to come closer. The girl stopped scribbling her notes and bounded over to Muffin's side, clearly excited that she was going to do something other than observe. "This is Fifi's first transition, so I'm going to have her take the reins while I observe. She's had training but hasn't had a chance to use her skills out in the wild as of yet."

"Oh." Charlotte tried to ignore the nervous, sinking feeling in her gut. Fifi didn't exactly look...trustworthy. For starters, her name was ridiculous, as was the poof of wild pink curls on her head. But Muffin seemed to know what she was doing, and she had an equally ridiculous name, so maybe things would be okay.

Muffin shuffled the heavy book over to Fifi, plopping it into the younger woman's arms. "You know what to do now, right, Fifi, my girl?"

Fifi nodded excitedly, juggling the book with one arm and flipping the pages with her other hand. "Which one are we doing again?"

"The Snow Queen. I thought I told you to write that down?" Muffin gave Charlotte a tight smile, as if to assuage her fears. "Perhaps you should close your eyes, dear. Wouldn't want you learning all of our trade secrets."

"Um, okay." That, and she wouldn't see that confused look on Fifi's face that was making her stomach feel like a block of ice. Charlotte squeezed her eyes shut and braced herself, waiting. As she did, she thought of her old life. Her parents, who would no doubt be devastated. Her friends, her coworkers, everyone wouldn't know what happened to her. They'd just know she was dead. A tear trickled down her cheek and she sniffed loudly.

"No crying," Muffin said in a kindly voice. "Everything's going to be all right. Just do what you have to in order to complete your task, and I'll take care of the rest, all right?"

Charlotte nodded, but she couldn't help it when a few more tears escaped. After all, she was justified in crying, she thought, considering that it wasn't every day that a girl died horribly in the dentist's chair. Wasn't she allowed a little self-pity?

Someone sneezed, and Charlotte heard the pages of the book rustle.

"Keep going," she heard Muffin whisper to Fifi. "You're doing just fine. Now raise your wand...there's a girl. Good job. Now up, and..."

A warm, misty air touched Charlotte's skin. It felt odd, but she didn't open her eyes lest she cause Fifi to lose control of her magic. Snow queen, she reminded herself. Defeat the snow queen and save the prince. Or...was he a prince? Maybe he was just a peasant. Whatever it was, she had to save the guy the snow queen had snatched. There couldn't be too many of those, could there? Save the guy, be the big damn hero. No problem.

Another tear slid down her cheek, and she raised a hand to brush it away...only to realize that the tear was frozen to her cheek.

"Oh, shit." Muffin said in a disgusted voice. "You've really done it now, Fifi."

Chapter Two

Charlotte opened her eyes and stared in dumbfounded wonder at the world around her. She stood in the midst of icy beauty. A courtyard unfurled before her, and everything was made of white snow and pearly blue-white ice. Flagstones of ice marked their way in a decorative path to the massive front doors of the castle. Trees were bare, their branches dripping with frosty icicles. The ground was covered in a pristine blanket of thick snow, and in the distance, spires of the ice castle rose before her. It looked like something out of a fairy tale...which made Charlotte laugh with delight. It was beautiful and didn't look fearsome at all.

But when she laughed, her breath puffed out into a cloud. Curious, Charlotte experimented, blowing her breath outward. Sure enough, it frosted mid-air, so beautiful and perfect that she could even see the snowflakes forming in the vapor.

Which was weird, because she wasn't cold in the slightest. Charlotte raised her arms, looking for goose-bumps...and noticed the pale bluish-white tinge of her skin. Her finger-tips were covered in frost.

Oh dear. "Um, I think we have a problem."

She turned to look at Fifi and Muffin, who stood behind her. The two women were frantically paging through the book, a guilty look on Fifi's face.

"But you said the Snow Queen," Fifi said, flipping the pages quickly, a warble in her voice that sounded as if she was going to start crying.

"I know I did," Muffin said in a too-patient voice that was at odds with the tight look on her wrinkled face. "Did you not hear the part where I said that the tale is called the Snow Queen but Charlotte will be playing the part of the heroine? *Not* the snow queen?"

"I might not have written that part down," Fifi mumbled.

"I'm the snow queen?" Charlotte glanced down at her pale, blue-tinged skin, at her frosted fingertips. She gazed down at her clothing, which seemed to have disappeared and been replaced with a spun confection of icicles and clouds of frost that served as puffs of skirt. She grabbed a handful of her hair - normally just a pale blonde - and found it, too, had been transformed. It was now the same milk white as the rest of her, the tips tinged with the frosty blue. Gorgeous. "I'm not supposed to be the bad guy, am I?"

Shame, because she was kind of getting a kick out of this. This whole snow queen thing was kinda cool, no pun intended.

"No, you're not," Muffin said in a firm voice. "You are supposed to be the heroine. Clearly someone was not paying attention."

Fifi looked abashed. It was like someone had kicked a puppy. "I messed up."

"It's okay," Charlotte told her soothingly. Poor kid. For all her weirdness, Fifi looked pretty young, and Muffin wasn't giving her the most understanding of looks. "Just wave your wand and switch me to the real one and we'll pretend this never happened."

14

"She can't," Muffin bit out, looking thoroughly exasperated. Her little apple cheeks were flushed bright red with emotion. "You have now been woven into the fabric as the snow queen, not the heroine. Once it's done, it's done."

Panic clutched at Charlotte. "I still get my second chance, right? You said I could have one."

"You do, but this is going into my progress report," Muffin said in a miffed tone. She clapped her hands together and shrugged. "Oh well. Nothing to be done about it now. Congratulations, my dear. You are now officially the snow queen."

"Thanks, I think?"

"Don't thank me just yet. You are now officially the antagonist of this story. Since you're no longer the heroine," she cast a disgruntled look at the quailing Fifi at her side, "the rules have changed a little. The heroine's going to be coming after you because you stole her man. I suppose you'll have to stop her if you want to win this fairy tale and turn the land into eternal frost or some such."

"Should I do that? Turn the land into eternal frost? That seems kind of...not nice."

Muffin shrugged. "You're not the nice guy. You stole the nice guy."

"Oh." Well, this was going to take some adjusting. Charlotte was one of those people that always tried to do the right thing - she never ran a red light, always tipped twenty percent, and never pushed ahead in line. She was going to be a horrible villain. She glanced over at Fifi, who looked ready to cry. Poor thing. "Well, I'll give it my best. I'm sure it'll be fine."

And she forced a smile to her face.

"All right, then. That's the spirit!" Muffin raised a hand to high-five her, and then lowered it. "Actually, I shouldn't touch you. Your skin will stick to mine."

15

"It will?" Charlotte stared at her hands. Other than being a wee bit paler than her normal self, she didn't look all that different, did she?

"Yes. You're a being composed of frost and magic, now. You can't touch normal humans, and normal temperatures will feel like a heat wave to you. I advise that you not head to the beach anytime soon."

"I was always more of an indoor girl," Charlotte joked. When Muffin didn't crack a smile, she sighed. "Really. It'll be okay. I'm sure I can be the snow queen just as easily as I can be the heroine."

Muffin nodded. "Good. Just remember. Keep that man away from the heroine at all costs and you win. You're the bad guy, so don't be afraid to do bad guy stuff if you need to."

Bad guy stuff? Charlotte didn't know if that was her thing. But she nodded. "No touching humans, avoid heat, and do whatever it takes to make sure I win. Got it."

"Fifi and I will stop by to check on things periodically," Muffin said, putting an arm around Fifi's shoulders. The pink fairy godmother intern seemed a little wilted under the heat of Muffin's disapproval, and she crossed her arms over her chest and shivered at the snowy weather. "We can't stay here long, so I'll just wish you good luck. Do you have anything else you want to ask before we leave?"

"Um, what exactly do I do with the captive guy?"

Muffin gave her a startlingly lewd wink. "You're the bad guy. Whatever you want."

And she and Fifi disappeared into a puff of smoke.

She was alone.

Charlotte glanced around the courtyard, chewing on her lip as she thought. Snow was falling in a heavy blanket, but it didn't bother her. Actually, the weather felt amazing. She glanced down at her warm feet and noticed they were not only bare, but six inches deep in drifting snow. She wiggled her toes in the powder and then shrugged.

Maybe being the snow queen would be simpler than she thought. Stick to the ice castle, hang out for a month, and drop the hero into the deepest darkest dungeon and hope for the best. Maybe she could make her ice castle more defensible. An ice maze? Who knew? Maybe she had some ice minions around her she could ask.

She...really should have asked for more details about this whole 'ice queen' thing before Muffin had disappeared. But at this point? Everything was starting to run together into a big blur in her mind. Her death, the weird fairy godmothers, the whole snow queen thing. Maybe that was why she wasn't more upset about dying - none of this felt like reality just yet.

Charlotte glanced at the cobblestone path made from ice crystals. She headed toward it and the icy cobbles felt like sun-warmed brick under her toes. Kinda delicious feeling. With a shiver of pleasure, she headed toward the frosty castle in the distance, noting the defenses of this place. There was a wall surrounding the ice castle, but it seemed more decorative than anything else, a spiraling, artful lattice of ice that could probably be snapped by a single hit with a baseball bat. If she was going to do this snow queen thing, she was going to do it right. She needed a thick wall around the castle. A moat, too. Maybe some spikes.

Just as soon as she figured out how to activate her powers, anyhow.

Charlotte extended her hands in front of her, considering. Was it like Iceman from the comic books, where she just extended her hands and ice would form? She tried it…and nothing happened. There was clearly a piece of the story missing here. Maybe someone around here would have answers.

Not that she'd seen anyone since arriving. The courtyard was empty, and she could sense no one nearby. Maybe she was the only one here? That'd be lonely. Still, beggars couldn't be choosers. And she did have at least one other person here.

She set off down the icy path toward her ice castle, intent on finding her captive.

As she approached the ice castle, she was continually amazed at how beautiful it was. The building was enormous, with delicate windows made from panes of wavy glass (that she suspected were ice) and tall, fluted spires that rose and twisted high into the cloudy skies. There were multiple towers, and the entire thing reminded her of an icy cousin to the famous Russian Kremlin.

The doors opened slowly as she went up the steps, as if attuned to her presence. Inside, she still saw no one. The interior was brightly lit despite having no visible light sources, and she suspected it was due to the ice and refracting of light. Or magic, she thought to herself. It could always have something to do with magic.

The walls of the palace were glittering and smooth, though when she looked closely, she could see delicate snowflake striations carved into the ice walls. There were no furnishings other than endless ice, but the ice seemed clever and flexible enough to provide everything that she needed, which was kind of neat on its own. Charlotte began opening doors just to see what was behind them, and she even found an icy sort of 'Snow Queen bathroom' which amused her to no end. There was a throne room (why, she had no idea, considering that the palace seemed devoid of subjects) and the throne was composed of ice so clear and smooth that it could have been made of glass.

Her bedroom was something out of a fantasy, that was for sure. Polar bear furs covered a raised dais, and Charlotte figured that must have been the bed. There were no personal adornments of any kind, no treasures or trinkets or anything to show a personal side to whoever the ice queen had been before. That was kind of odd...or sad. Did the snow queen not bother with personal items? Or had they all been removed prior to Charlotte's arrival? More questions that she didn't have an answer to.

At the far end of her chambers, though, she spotted a large mirror and nearly fell over in shock at her own reflection. Stunned, she approached the mirror, her hand going to her mouth and touching it, if only to see the person in the mirror do the same and know it was her reflection she was looking at.

She was...gorgeous.

Her skin was porcelain pale and perfect. And while it was her own face that stared back at her, it was like she'd been converted into this whole 'Snow Queen' thing from head to toe. Her hair hung in glossy, white-blue waves and tumbled around her shoulders, and her brows were a darker bluish shade that framed her blue eyes quite well. Her lashes were long and spiky with white, and her lips held just a hint of blue tint to them. There was no longer a hint of pink in her coloring. On a whim, she tugged at the front of her icicle bodice and glanced down at her breasts.

Blue nipples.

"You have *got* to be kidding me," Charlotte muttered aloud, and then was hit with a fit of the giggles. This had definitely crossed over into the realm of absurdity.

She admired her reflection for a moment longer, especially the inventiveness of her icicle-and-frost dress, when she noticed two small chips missing out of the corner of the mirror. Frowning, she moved forward and examined it. Broken?

As she touched the mirror, she felt a shiver of unease, as if dark things were brushing against her mind.

Startled, Charlotte jerked her hand away. What was with this mirror? She peered into it, and the longer she stared, the creepier it seemed. Her own reflection seemed to distort as she gazed at it.

Just then, she heard a low groan somewhere in the distance.

Charlotte froze and backed away from the mirror, looking around. "Who's there?"

No response. Had it been her imagination? Maybe the ice castle was settling and the ice was groaning as it shifted? Did ice do that? She'd seen no one so far.

Of course, she was also supposed to have a guy held captive somewhere around here and she hadn't seen him yet. Maybe this was her cue.

Charlotte gave one last uneasy glance to the mirror and examined the gleaming walls of her chamber. That had sounded awfully close, but she hadn't seen any doors except for the main one that she'd come through. Was there a hidden chamber somewhere? She touched a wall and it felt warm, despite looking like sub-zero ice. It also felt completely smooth - if there was a door, she couldn't see one. Frowning to herself, Charlotte moved along the chamber, her hands skimming the walls. "Hello out there," she called. "If you can hear me, can you make another sound?"

Another groan, and this one sounded almost as if it were beneath her feet. Curious, Charlotte glanced down at the gleaming floors...and gasped. A shadow deep beneath the glassy ice moved, just a bit.

Someone was down there.

She looked around anxiously. There was an enormously large polar bear skin covering the floor next to her bed - so large that it was a little alarming to think it had come from a real animal. On a hunch, she lifted one corner of the blanket, and saw a trap door.

Not the cleverest queen out there, Charlotte thought to herself. But she supposed that was a good thing, or else she might never have found him. "I'm coming," she called out, and shoved the rug aside, then lifted the trap door, easing it backward. A set of glossy ice stairs met her eyes, twisting down into the bluish light of the chamber below her own.

Charlotte went down the steps carefully, wishing she had a torch for light - one pitfall of being a snow queen, she supposed. The shadows grew deeper here, the muted blues and silvers of the ice gleaming around her. Her heart began to pound furiously in her chest, uncertain at what she might find. She stepped off of the last stair delicately, her gaze going to a series of massive icy spikes forming a prison at the far end of the shadowy chamber. Oh dear. "Hello?"

"Mistress," a voice rasped. "Please."

Oh no. Was he being tortured? She rushed forward, unable to see anything beyond the icy barrier. Her hand went to the ice and she pushed at it, hoping for a door to magically appear and swing backward. Instead, the ice melted under her hand, flowing and ebbing backward like the tide. Was that how her power worked? She had to touch the ice and mentally demand something? Fascinated, Charlotte continued to push at the ice until she had cleared a small gateway for her to step through. Maybe she was going to get the hang of this after all.

But as the ice melted away, she caught a glimpse of the man.

And stopped in shock.

He was naked. Really naked. Really, really naked. Bronzed skin stood out like a stain against all the delicate silvers and blues of her icy palace. His flesh was rippling with good health and a thick dose of muscle. Thick, muscular arms were pinned backward and bound behind him with a pair of icy cuffs, and his feet were bound exactly the same. A delicate chain pulled between the two, more or less keeping him hog-tied in the dungeon. He was hunched over on a scatter of straw, and only the flexing of one very large bronze thigh kept her from seeing his full nudity. Black hair hung messily over his face and played at his nape, a bit longer than she was used to seeing on a man. His eyes were covered with a strip of ice that served as a blindfold, and everywhere the ice touched him, his skin was reddened underneath.

Charlotte swallowed hard. This…did not look like the actions of a very nice person. For the first time, she was starting to comprehend exactly what being the 'snow queen' meant. She *was* the bad guy. "Hello?"

The man's head lifted and Charlotte got a good look at his face. Oh, sweet lord. No wonder the snow queen had stolen this man. He was the most gorgeous creature she'd ever seen. She couldn't see his eyes underneath all that ice, but the planes of his face were well sculpted, his nose elegant, and his mouth incredibly sensual. A scruff of black beard curved his jaw, and Charlotte guessed that 'shaving' wasn't a priority for the snow queen's prisoners.

He shifted, trying to get to his feet, and landed heavily on his knees instead. As he did, she saw that he'd been bound in another way, as well. Ice covered his genitals and they had been frozen into a state of arousal. Oh. Oh dear. Boy, this snow queen was a piece of work, wasn't she?

"Mistress," he said in a low voice, and she watched the ice on his groin stir, as if fighting his erection. Oh, awkward.

"Um, are you okay?"

"I ache to touch you, mistress. Please, let me free."

Uh, okay. There was something weird in his voice when he said that. Almost monotone. "You can't touch me. At least, I'm pretty sure you can't. I'm all icy and stuff."

"You said the burn would only convince you of my love."

"Did I say that?" Yikes. She moved forward, careful to avoid brushing him with her skirts, and examined his face. The ice covering his eyes was shaped almost like glasses. Could she take it off somehow without hurting him? Experimentally, she held her palm close to his skin. His rose with gooseflesh even as her own felt as if she were holding it close to a fire. Okay, that wouldn't be good. Definitely no touching. Yet even as she did, she felt him lean toward her touch, and she was barely able to pull away before she accidentally hurt him.

He groaned when she pulled away.

This was weird. Why keep the guy captive like this if he was in love with her? It didn't make sense. "Hold still," she told him. She couldn't leave him like this.

Gently, using only her fingertips, she touched the icy mask and concentrated. The ice ebbed under her fingertips, parting from his eyes and turning to liquid. It ran down his cheeks like tears and he blinked for a moment, dark, spiky lashes fluttering.

Then, he opened his eyes. They were entirely silver, gleaming like mirrors. She could see no pupils in them. How...weird.

"Hi," she told him. "What's your name?"

"You know my name, Mistress," he said in that same weird tone of voice. It was almost like the words were being pulled out of him against his will. "I am Kai."

"I'm going to free you now, Kai," she told him. "Just stay still and don't move, okay?"

"You will free me and then we will make love?" Those weird mirrored eyes followed her.

"Um, no?" Good lord, was this guy brainwashed? Or was the snow queen really that good in bed that this guy wanted to bang her despite her iciness? A hot blush crept over her cheeks at the thought. Yeah, she was definitely the wrong girl for this job. Every prior boyfriend had thought she was frigid. Oh, the irony. "This just looks really uncomfortable and it seems unfair to you, so I'm going to free you."

"Yes, mistress," he intoned.

"Stay still."

He went deathly still, so unmoving that he could have been a statue. Yet another unnerving thing about this situation. The whole thing was downright weird. Charlotte moved forward and gently touched the cuffs at his hands, working them until she felt her fingertips tingle and the ice melted. He didn't move even though he was freed, and she winced at the condition of his wrists. The skin there was blistered from the cold, bright red and chafed. It looked painful.

And speaking of painful...she glanced at Kai's front, and the cock that stabbed forward, encased in ice. Yowch. That did not look like fun at all. Of course, she had to take it off of him...which meant giving him a rather intimate touch.

She glanced up at Kai's mirrored eyes and noticed he was watching her, though he'd remained totally still. That blush she felt on her cheeks grew even hotter, and she could hear the crackle of the ice that she'd melted as it refroze. Okay, when her body temperature went up, the temperature of the air around her seemed to go down. Good to know. Even Kai's bronze skin was dotted with goose-bumps. She forced herself to relax, and then looked Kai in the eyes. "I'm, uh, going to take care of that." She pointed primly at his groin. "So it's imperative

24

that you don't move or something might get burned, okay?"

"I will remain still," he said, his voice husky.

"Great," she told him, and knelt in front of him. He was much bigger than her. Now that she was kneeling in front of him, she had an idea of just how big this man was. Her head came up to his shoulder, and his torso was as big as a tree trunk. They sure grew them big around here.

Her gaze fell to the icy branch of his cock, and her cheeks flushed again. Definitely grew them big. She considered the best way to remove it without being weird about it, and then determined that there was really no way to do so. Best to just get it over with. Sucking in a breath, Charlotte laid her palm on the tip of the ice, and then encircled his thick length with her hand. She stroked downward, easing her magic through the ice.

He groaned.

She snatched her hand away, mortified. That hadn't been a groan of pain like before. That had been one of...pleasure. Oh, mercy. Heat began to pulse, low through her pelvis. What kind of sick woman was she that trying to free this poor man was going to turn her on? "I'm so sorry," she told him. "There's no other way to do this."

And she placed her hand on him again. Her own breathing was becoming raspy with that sick sort of excitement, and she stroked her hand down the ice again, watching as it melted away from his cock. At least he wasn't blistered there, she told herself with relief, though his skin was reddened. A bead of pre-cum glistened on the head of his cock...and then didn't slide down his skin. It froze there instead. Her arousal was making the room incredibly cold.

Charlotte looked up at the man, her breathing heavy, and noticed that those mirrored eyes were still watching her with fascination. "Sorry about that," she told him. "It couldn't be helped."

"Will you not keep touching me?"

She shook her head, backing away a step. "It's...it's not right. I'm sorry." She moved to his feet and melted the cuffs there, without saying another word. When she was done, he remained still. "Can you walk around?"

He got to his feet, rising to his full height, and Charlotte blinked, staring up at him. She was an average woman - or at least she had been - but next to this man, she felt positively dainty. He towered over her, all muscles and bronze skin, and she forced herself to keep her gaze on his face so things wouldn't get weird, considering he wasn't wearing anything.

"I'm very sorry about all that," she told him.

"I had displeased you," he told her in that monotone. "I deserved the punishment you gave me."

"I'm not sure about that." Charlotte chewed on her lip, thinking. There was still something really off about all of this. Kai was a bit weird, but the man acted like he wanted to jump her bones, not escape. Wasn't this supposed to be more difficult? Or was this truly supposed to be this easy? She didn't know, and Muffin hadn't exactly left her a training manual. For the first time, she wished she'd paid more attention to fairy tales. Who knew that she'd be forced to interact in one at a later date? "Do you have any more ice anywhere else?" She could feel her cheeks blushing even as she asked it. "Anywhere I can't see?"

"I do not."

There was something about this still bothering her, though. She examined his face, and his strange mirrored eyes. Something gleamed in the corner of each one. Something shiny and unnatural. "Did I do something to your eyes?"

"Yes, mistress."

Damn it. "Lean down."

He did, and she got all disconcerted at the sight of him leaning in close. He really was beautiful, even if his warmth did feel a bit like standing in front of an inferno. Those strange eyes watched her, his face so close to hers that she would have felt his breath…but she realized he was holding it. Thinking of her, perhaps?

She studied his face. There was definitely something shiny in the corner of each eye. "I'm sorry," she warned him. "But I'm going to have to touch you."

"I await your touch with anticipation, mistress."

"You won't be saying that when I stick a finger in your eye," she grumbled, but moved forward. She extended one finger close to the corner of his eye, and to her surprise, before she could touch him, the shiny object flew out of his eye and landed on her fingertip as if magnetized. She stared at it. It looked like a chip of mirror.

The mirror in her room had been missing two chips. "What in the world?" She glanced back at Kai and noticed that his eye was a dark amber-brown now, with a normal pupil. Her fingertip went to the other one and the mirror chip flew out before she could touch him again. She frowned at the twin chips in her hand, and then patted her dress, looking for a pocket. When she didn't find one, she shrugged and slid the chips into her bodice. "Strange stuff, Kai. Do you feel better now?"

He didn't answer.

She looked up at his face.

His beautiful mouth was twisted into a snarl, and those amber-brown eyes flickered with emotion. Rage. He bared his teeth in a grimace and lunged at her.

Charlotte barely was able to duck and sidestep as he went flying past her, skidding on the icy floors that caused her bare feet no trouble. He slammed into one of the nearby walls, and cursed under his breath. Then, he turned, big shoulders heaving. "Monster," he growled. "I'll have your heart."

Her eyes widened. "Kai?"

"You have not earned the right to address me, foul creature!" He lunged at her again, big body launching from the icy wall toward her.

She gave a shriek of surprise and threw a hand up to protect herself, flinching away. She braced herself for the impact of his massive body on hers...but it never came. Instead, she heard a crackle of ice, and her eyes opened a moment later in surprise. When she'd thrown her arm up, she'd created an ice barrier, and it had protected her from Kai's lunge. The barrier had shattered under the force of his weight, and he'd rolled to the floor, where he was even now picking himself up off the ground for yet another attack, his handsome face drawn into a rictus of anger.

Completely gone was the Kai that had begged her to touch him in that weird monotone. The man that stood before her now was huge and enraged.

"Stop it," she told him in a quaking voice. "I just freed you!"

That brought a snarl to his lips. "Yes, you freed me for more of your sick, twisted games. Games that I want no part of. You will have to enchant me again if you wish me pliable, foul woman."

Enchant him again?

The mirror shards in her bodice. Of course. No wonder he'd been so weirdly compliant. She shook her head and darted to the side even as he ran for her again.

She didn't move fast enough; he grabbed her ankle even as he leapt and both of them slammed to the ground. Charlotte's chin smacked into the floor, and the breath escaped her with a whoosh. A searing pain shot up her leg, and she cried out, kicking at his grip. He refused to release her, though, his teeth gritted even as her skin smoked as if she were being burned.

"Let me go!"

"You were not saying that yesterday," he told her in a hard, sneering voice.

"Things...change!" She kicked at his face, her bare foot connecting with his jaw. Both of them yelped at the skin contact, and to her relief, he released her throbbing ankle. She scrambled away, crawling across the floors on all fours.

She heard him scrambling behind her, and knew he was going to grab her again if she didn't think fast. So she did - she flattened her palm and smacked it, hard, against the icy floor.

The entire room jumped as the ice responded to her, and spikes shot up into the air around her, growing into massive protective icicles in the space of mere seconds. They surrounded her like a small fortress, glittering and dangerous.

Kai snarled his rage and punched at the icicles from the other side, but she immediately repaired them as soon as he did. He wouldn't be able to get to her.

Charlotte exhaled in relief, her heart racing. What the hell had just happened? The queen had clearly been keeping Kai enchanted and pliable - and he had hated every moment of it. He'd just tried to kill her. She swallowed hard and sat up in her little icy fortress, glaring at him from behind the safety of her spiky icicles. "That wasn't very nice."

"I have no time for nice," he sneered.

She curled her legs close and hissed at the bright red welt encircling her ankle. It hurt like a burn where he'd touched her. How could the snow queen be sexually interested in a man when it scalded her to touch him? Sick. No wonder Kai hated her.

She glanced up at him...and noticed he was no longer glaring down at her. Instead, he was racing to the steps, determined to escape. Crap! She laid both of her hands on the ice floor and visualized it wrapping around Kai's feet and sucking him down. Sure enough, she felt the flooring ripple and a scarce moment later, before Kai could touch the bottom step, the floor wrapped around his feet and halted him in his tracks.

No wonder the snow queen lived in an ice palace ‑ everything and anything was a weapon.

Kai yanked furiously at his legs. "Let me go!"

"I can't."

He gave her an angry glare, still jerking at his legs. "Set me free and I vow to you that I and my kin will never set foot in your lands again."

Charlotte sighed. "I really wish I could, but I can't. You have to stay here with me." She wiggled her fingertips against the ice, and watched it ripple and surf like a wave, gently dragging him back to his bed in the corner, even as he was helpless to move. She had him trapped. Poor guy. "It's for the best if you stay here, and since you're going to try and escape, I have no choice but to leave you locked up."

She dumped him in the straw. A moment later, she reformed the icicle fortress around him instead of around herself, trapping him there.

"You cannot keep me here," he roared furiously.

"I don't have a choice, and neither do you,' she told him in a pert voice. "So just get used to it."

Chapter Three

Curse the evil woman.

Kai shivered in his cell, furious at the queen. And furious at himself, really. It was his fault that he'd been captured again. He didn't know what had possessed her, but when she took the mirror-shards out of his eyes that kept him enchanted and complacent, he should have killed her. Planted his hands on the sides of that delicate jaw and twisted until he heard her neck snap.

But he hadn't. Instead, he'd hesitated while she stared up at him so pretty and soft.

And that hesitation had cost him.

It was a mistake he'd made twice now. The first time, when he'd seen her in the snowy woods and she'd looked so regal and pale. He'd been struck dumb by her, and hadn't known who she was until she'd touched him and placed the magic shards in his eyes.

And then he'd found out. He'd been helpless to disagree even as she'd stolen him away from his village, taken him to her icy keep, and then amused herself by finding new and ghoulish ways to torture him. She was attracted to him - that much was obvious - but because she couldn't touch him without burning herself, she settled for torturing him and arousing him against his

31

will. That had been part of the spell - to make him lust for her no matter what awful things she did. Even when she stabbed him with icicles or brushed her burning fingers against his cock? He'd still wanted her even though he despised her with every ounce of his being. She'd known he'd despised her, too, and simply hadn't cared. She'd simply smirked at every monotone "Yes, I want you more than anything, Mistress." She'd known the truth behind those words, and loved to make him say them.

It was just another way to break him. She did love her games.

Today must have been a new game, Kai decided as he huddled on the straw and pulled his legs close to conserve body heat. She had tired of being the hard, cruel snow queen and decided to go with a slightly different tactic. When she'd arrived today, she'd been soft and sweet, her words half amused and half chagrined. The little fluttering touches she'd made, careful not to brush his skin, had been achingly sweet. And when she'd reached for his cock and stroked the ice off of it? There'd been a pretty bluish tint to her pale cheeks that told him that she was blushing like a virgin.

It had made him hard...and it had made him despise himself. This was just another game, and she excelled at messing with his mind.

She was an excellent actress, too. She'd pulled out the ice shards and had acted as if she'd had no clue what they were. She'd looked shocked and hurt when he'd attacked her. Even her overall demeanor had changed - she was somehow softer, less cruel. Less brittle around the edges. The hard, cunning look in her eyes was gone. When she smiled, it looked as if she'd meant it.

So of course, he knew it was a ruse. And he hated that his body had responded to it. Was he that desperate for a woman's touch that he'd welcome the icy caress of his enemy?

He was betrothed to Gerda, his childhood friend and playmate. And while there wasn't love between them, there was respect and friendship. Never unabashed lust like he felt for the beautiful, fragile-yet-strong snow queen.

And he hated that more than anything. It should be Gerda that filled his dreams at night, not a demon with blue-tipped fingernails and silky, white-blonde waves of hair.

The trap door opened above, and he tensed, getting to his feet. He forced himself to stand tall and proud, despite the chill in the air and the pain shooting through his weary muscles. He was starving, too, but he wouldn't ask her for food. He'd learned weeks ago that she liked to withhold anything he asked for, so he'd learned not to ask for anything.

Footsteps. A moment later, she came into view, the polar bear skins that normally covered her lush bed in her arms. To his surprise, she dropped them on the floor and then picked up the first one, bundling it in her arms and then lobbing it over the ice.

It landed at his feet with a splat. He made no attempt to touch it, only watched her.

She tossed the next one over, as well. And then the final one. When he didn't move a muscle, she frowned. "Aren't you cold?"

He was; he'd never admit it to her. So he said nothing.

She moved closer to his prison, and that blush stole up her cheeks again. He watched as she raised a hand to shield her eyes, and carefully avoided looking at his nudity. "Do you have any pants? I can get them if you can tell me where they are."

Kai's eyes narrowed. Was this a trick? Get him to admit that he desperately wanted clothing and then withhold it from him? Worse, dress him in female garb and make him beg for favors? Humiliate him?

She looked sad that he wouldn't respond. "You're not going to talk to me, are you?"

"I have nothing to say to you, Snow Queen."

She chewed on her lip. "Boy, they weren't kidding when they said this bad guy thing would be a challenge." She tilted her head, staring at him, then said, "You don't have to call me 'Snow Queen'. My name is Charlotte. Charlotte Ross."

"You have already coerced my name from me," he said coldly. "What more do you want?"

She sighed. "A conversation? You're the only one here."

He said nothing.

"Have it your way," she told him, and then waved a hand at the polar bear skins. "I brought those because I thought you might be cold. It...It's not cold here for me. Feels a little warm, actually." She rubbed her hands along her bare arms in a surprisingly sensual gesture that he'd never seen her do before. Her fingers trailed over that milky pale skin, and gods help him, he watched her with fascination, remembering those frost-tipped fingertips as they stroked his iced-over cock, and the way her gaze had shyly met his. "Anyhow, I'll look for some pants. If I find you some, I'll bring them, I promise. No bargaining required."

When he continued to remain silent, she gave another unhappy little sigh. She turned and left, and he was alone with the polar bear skins. He hesitated a long moment, not sure if this was yet another test. But when she didn't return, he grasped one and then threw it around his shoulders, burrowing into the warmth.

If her goal was to confuse him, she'd succeeded admirably. Kai was downright baffled by her change of heart.

It was the first night that Kai had slept comfortably since arriving at the snow queen's palace. While it was cold, it wasn't so bone-numbingly chilly that he couldn't function. Her furs had helped, though it had bothered him that they'd smelled sweet and clean, like she did. Evil shouldn't smell so wholesome, he thought to himself.

She returned the next day with a small pack. His pack, he noticed, identifying the buckskin fringe and beadwork as that of his tribe's. He willed himself not to get too excited, though, waiting for her to make the first move.

"I found this," she said in a soft voice, moving toward the bars of his icy prison. She held it up for him to see. "There's some sort of food inside." She played with the fringe with long, delicate fingers, and he abruptly thought of her hand on his cock again - and wished he hadn't. "I suppose this is yours?"

He gritted his teeth and forced himself not to respond, not to reach through the bars and snatch it back from her.

"It's okay," she said. "I can tell from the way you're glaring at me that it must be yours. You seem to have an extra-special amount of hate right now. The question is, what do I do with this bag?" She held it out to him and considered, then drew it back.

And here begin the games, he thought with fury. Now she would make it clear what she was after. More torture? Sexual pleasure? Both?

"I'd like for you to say my name," she said in a soft voice. "Please."

It was that 'please' that got him. It was something she'd never said before. "You are Charlotte Ross."

She exhaled, the sound almost relieved. "I am. It's good to hear someone else say it."

Now what did that mean? "You are also the snow queen," he added in a flat voice.

She looked sad. "Only because I have to be. I didn't choose it. I was supposed to be the heroine."

What on earth was she talking about? She made no sense.

She sighed and handed the bag over to him, sticking her hand through the icicles. He could have grabbed her wrist and slammed her into the ice. He could have hauled her against it, or at the very least, snapped her arm. The look in her eyes said she knew all these things and was still taking that chance.

Kai took the bag from her grasp and gave her a stiff nod of acknowledgement.

A soft, sweet smile curved her face. "You're welcome."

Being the snow queen was boring.

She'd been here for two days. Kai still didn't talk to her - not that she blamed him. No one else was around. There was no TV, no radio, no nothing but endless ice and snow and her pretty - if lonely - castle. At first she'd found it fascinating, but after two days of nothing but ice? She was bored out of her mind.

Well...almost.

She'd explored when she'd first arrived. The castle seemed to have endless passageways and hidden nooks and crannies that she could feel underneath the ice. It was like all she had to do was touch the ice and she'd know what was on the other side. The old snow queen liked her secrets, apparently, and had a hidden library, a laboratory of things that Charlotte knew nothing about, and a secret, hidden room deep beneath the rest of the keep that held the creepy mirror.

She'd been bored by the books in the library, unable to read any of them. She'd cleaned up the laboratory and threw out anything that looked vaguely like eye of newt or wing of bat. That wasn't her jig, evil queen abilities or not.

But the room with the mirror? That shit freaked her out.

Bad.

The thing oozed magic. And not good, clean, wholesome magic. It oozed magic that made her want to take a shower or wash her hands. It made her feel dirty just to be in its presence. More than that, she felt watched when she stood in front of it, almost like there was someone else in the room. She'd been unable to sleep the first night, not with it in the room. So she'd covered it in ice that way she didn't have to look into it, and toted it to one of the secret rooms, far in the back of the palace.

And she'd abandoned it there. She was pretty sure the mirror was pissed about that, too. Every time she went through that area, she got a creepy vibe. Once, she was pretty sure she heard someone whisper her name.

Yeah, no thanks.

Unnerved, she erected another ice wall around the mirror room just because it made her feel better.

The rest of the castle felt safe, though. And now that she had figured out how to use her powers, though, she'd set about fortifying the castle. Gone was the delicately wrought gate that looked as if it could break with one well-placed finger. Instead, it was a slab of solid ice, with spikes covering it from the outside. She'd been building the walls, too, turning the delicate, piped confections into something more monstrous and scary. It took a lot of ice and snow, and by the time she'd done no more than a foot, she was exhausted. But she didn't have anything else to do, and the girl that was coming - the heroine of this fairy tale - was determined to kill her, so it was time well spent, Charlotte figured. So she worked herself into exhaustion and collapsed into her frosty bed each night.

But it was still boring, quiet work, and it left her with nothing but her own internal thoughts. And those? Were kind of a mess at the moment. Chalk it up to the whole 'death' or 'bad guy' thing or just everything all at once? She wasn't handling this well. She was lonely and unhappy. The only other person here was Kai and he hated her guts.

Everyone hated her. She was the bad guy.

Charlotte ate her dinner alone every night. Magical, flavored cubes of snow appeared on a dainty plate every evening. That made sense, considering her body temperature was more or less absolute zero. She ate them, even though she didn't know what was in them or who delivered them. It could have been magic and she was all alone, or it could have been unseen servants that avoided her because they thought she was awful. Either one depressed her.

She was sitting in her lonely throne, her small table at her side, and feeling more than a little sorry for herself. She was exhausted and unhappy, and she still had 28 days to go before she would win this thing.

Even bad company was still company, she decided, and took her small plate to her bedroom and opened the trap door to go visit Kai.

He got to his feet as she descended the stairs, his entire stance wary. She tried smiling at him, but it faltered. So instead, she just touched the wall and dragged out enough ice to make a small stool, sat down, perched her plate on her knees, and began to eat.

Kai said nothing, though eventually he relaxed enough to squat on his heels, still watching her. She was pleased to see that he was wrapped in the polar bear skins she'd left him.

"How's it going?" She asked, keeping her tone light so he couldn't tell just how despairing she was.

"How is what going?"

"You know, how has your day been?"

He stared at her as if she were crazy. "I have been trapped in a cage of your design. How exactly should my day be going?"

"You don't have to be so touchy," she said with a small sigh. "Have you been in the cage long?"

"You should know. You put me here."

"Let's say I can't remember because I don't keep track of days." She waved a hand idly. "Snow Queen biz and all. How many days have you counted?"

He hesitated for a long moment, then said, "Sixty."

Sixty? God, that was cruel. "I'm really sorry."

He gave her an incredulous look, and then snorted.

Well, that made her feel worse. "It's true. You don't have to believe me, but I am sorry. None of this was my idea."

"Then let me go."

Well, she couldn't do that, either. Charlotte shook her head, looking sadly at him. "I have to keep you here with me. It's part of the plan."

"Plan?" His lip curled derisively. "What plan?"

It was clear he didn't believe her, and she suspected telling him all about how she'd died and been replaced into the wrong person? Probably wouldn't go over so well, either. "Never mind." She shoved another flavored cube into her mouth and chewed slowly, miserable. She glanced up at Kai again. "You've been here two months. Have you seen anyone else?"

He stared at her, as if not quite believing her questions. Then he shook his head. "You told me once that you forbade anyone to visit you. That you preferred your privacy."

"Did I?" Charlotte sighed at that. "That sounds rotten, so that sounds like me. Unfortunately." She popped another cube into her mouth, disgruntled. "I kind of suck."

He reached for an icicle, then drew a hand back. "You should let me go."

"I wish I could. Unfortunately, you're stuck with me."

"Why?"

"Can't say?"

"What is it you plan to do with me?"

She considered this. "Hold on to you for another month."

He looked surprised by her answer, studying her with a puzzled expression. "For what purpose?"

"You wouldn't believe me if I told you," she said. "Then I suppose I'll go back to whatever it is that snow queens do with their spare time." She fiddled with one of the cubes. "I don't suppose you know what I had planned?"

He narrowed his eyes at her. "You don't know?"

She had no clue, actually. But since some of the other things she'd discovered about the snow queen had been not so nice, she was curious in a rather nauseated sort of way. "Humor me?"

"You told me," he began slowly, watching her reaction, "that you intended on turning the entire realm into one of ice and snow, and subjugating those that wouldn't follow your rule."

Charlotte considered this. "Sounds ambitious."

He said nothing, simply regarded her with that suspicious expression.

"Did I mention how, exactly, I'm going to do that?"

"You arrived here three months ago. Ever since then, our lands have been swept into an endless winter. As long as you remain here, you will continue to destroy everything."

So she was winning simply by being present? That was easy. She considered the ramifications of eternal winter. Nothing but snow and ice, which was fine for her, of course, but everyone and everything would starve. Plants would die and so would all the livestock that depended on them, and then the humans. She'd be a mass murderer, and all she'd have to do is sit back and encourage the snow. Lovely. "Doesn't seem like the nicest thing to do."

He laughed then, the sound hard and brittle. "Since when have you cared about doing the nice thing? Ever since you arrived you have attacked others and destroyed lives. You stole me from my people and have used me for your own cruel whims. And now you have a change of heart? You'll forgive me if I don't quite believe your tales, Cold One."

"No, I don't guess you would." She wasn't surprised by that, not really. He hated her, and she couldn't blame him. Apparently the snow queen had been quite awful to him. She wondered - not for the first time - what those cruel whims had been. Then she thought of the ice on his groin and blushed. She could guess some of them.

"Why are you here, asking me these things?" He sounded as if he hated her being here.

It made Charlotte even sadder. She shrugged, trying not to take it to heart. She wasn't this awful Snow Queen. She wasn't. She was just time-sharing her body for a time. That was all. And she couldn't let this get to her. "I just wanted someone to talk to, that's all. I miss having friends."

"Friends?" he echoed. "What does a creature like you need with friends?"

She was beginning to wonder the same thing. Perhaps Muffin had set her up for the loneliest challenge of all, and the real trick wouldn't be keeping the heroine from Kai, but keeping her own wits about her through this ordeal.

She had something up her sleeve.

Kai couldn't figure her out. This had to be some sort of new trick to get him to let down his guard. Being hard and cruel might have been fun for her in the beginning, but it was obvious she'd lost her enthusiasm for it and decided to try a different tactic. It had to be why she kept showing up, eating her meals with him and asking him bizarre questions.

It had to be why she had that sad, desperate look in her big blue eyes.

She was clever, too. She thought of everything. When she visited him, she acted as if she hated his cage almost as much as he did. She asked him soft questions about himself. How old was he? What were his people like? What did his food taste like? Was he warm enough? Did he have enough food? Would he like a bath?

And when it was late at night and she was up in her bed, he could have sworn that he'd heard the soft sound of distressed weeping.

Kai was beginning to miss the cruel side of the snow queen. At least that, he understood. Removing the enchantment that kept him complacent and then trying to befriend him? This was clearly part of a game, but one he couldn't figure out. And he didn't like that.

After a day or two of this, he decided to use her games against her. She pretended to be lonely? He'd be friendly to her. Attentive. Caring. She wanted a friend? He'd be that friend. And then when she let her guard down, he'd destroy her.

She was not the only that could be a cold, calculating liar. And she'd soon learn that he could be just as ruthless as she.

As she'd begun to do every day, she showed up after the sun had set and the night grew cold. She looked weary, dark circles under her bright blue eyes, and when she drew ice up from the floor to create her stool, it seemed to take her longer than usual.

He took bites of his travel bread from his pack - the last of it - as he watched her. Now she was showing weakness in front of him? Another ploy? Very well; he'd play along. "You look fatigued," he commented between bites. "Not sleeping?"

She looked utterly surprised that he'd addressed her first, and then pleased. A soft, shy smile crossed her face, so sweet that he'd almost believed it. "No. I have a hard time falling asleep, I suppose. Too much on my mind."

"Do you need your blankets back?" he gestured at one of the furs wrapped around him.

She shook her head. "I know this is an ice castle, but it feels warm to me - over-warm, really." She wiped her brow and he noticed for the first time that it gleamed with perspiration. "They'll do you far more good than me."

"Thank you," he told her, keeping the venom out of his voice. He felt a stab of excitement when she gave him another surprised, but pleased look.

"You're talking to me."

"As you've said, there is no one else to talk to."

This time, the smile that curved her face was wry. "I know you don't like me."

"You are being kind to me," he told her, though the words galled him even as they passed his lips. "I can appreciate that." He tapped a fingernail on the hard icicles that made the bars of his cage. "Even if I don't appreciate this."

She looked just as unhappy at the bars as he felt. "Necessity, I'm afraid." And she set that little tray of colored cubes in her lap and began to eat.

He needed to get her attention again. "I'm almost out of food," he said, and shook his empty pouch at her.

"Oh." Her pale white brows drew together. She offered him her tray of colored cubes. "Can you eat these?"

"I don't know. I've never tried them. You've never offered them to me before."

She got to her feet, tray in her hands, and approached his cell. The icicles were too thick and closely formed to be able to wedge the tray through, which he knew. She picked up one of the cubes and held it out to him between delicate, frost-tipped fingers, and then pulled her hand back, considering. "I don't know if this is too cold for you."

He shrugged.

She seemed mystified, though, and disappointed as she placed the cube back on the tray. "I don't want to burn you when I'm trying to give you a treat."

"If you want to treat me, Queen, let me out."

"Please," she murmured, shaking her head. "Call me by my real name."

"Charlotte," he said, though it tasted strange in his mouth. "Let me out."

"I wish I could." That wistful look crossed her face again. "I can't, though. It's not part of the plan. What do I normally feed you?"

Did she hit her head? Was that why she kept asking him such strange questions? Or did she lose her memory the more she used her power? When he'd first arrived, she'd only used her powers for small, selfish little whims — such as torturing him with ice. He'd grown to dread the slight crackle that came from the icy floors as she'd passed, the magical domain responding to her. Over the past few days, though, she'd been expelling a great deal of magic - the castle had been filled with the subtle, constant crackles of ice being manipulated. Not for the first time, he wondered what she'd been up to.

So he decided to test something.

"Why not let me out as you did before?" he lied. "So we can have dinner together once more, like friends instead of mistress and slave."

They'd never had dinner together like that. She'd kept him bound and confined, and when he wasn't forced to kneel at her feet like a dog, she'd kept him locked away in his cell. But he was curious to see how she'd react to his blatant lie.

The snow queen considered this for a long, long moment, her pale gaze holding him. He scarcely dared to breathe, waiting for her cruel smile to curve that beautiful mouth into hardness, for her to let on that she was well aware of his game.

But instead, all she said was, "I'd like to do that...but I don't trust you not to run."

"Ice the doors," he said quickly. "Then I won't be able to escape your chambers."

She paused.

"You know you can quickly overtake me again. You certainly stopped me fast the other day," he cajoled, his voice soothing and low. "Your ice powers are beyond my mere human strength."

After a long moment, she nodded. She set the tray down in her ice-chair and then climbed the stairs. "Be right back."

He watched her go, dumbfounded.

He'd lied to her. Told her that she'd let him roam freely in the past...and she'd accepted it? As if it was the truth?

This...wasn't right. Something was wrong.

Had she truly lost her memory? Maybe all the use of her powers fragmented her thoughts? He didn't know. All he knew was that she'd somehow changed a few days ago.

And he intended on taking advantage of it.

She returned a short time later, wiping her brow, now frosted with perspiration. "The doors are iced," she said. "Three feet thick. It'd take you hours to escape if you tried to break through, and if you kill me, this place will collapse around your ears. The entire ice palace is only held together by my magic."

He studied her to see if she was bluffing, but her delicate face was expressionless. "Fair enough," he said slowly, thinking. He wouldn't kill her, then. At least, not right away. He'd wait until her guard was down. He'd have to convince her to take him out of the castle, somehow. Then, when she was relaxed in his presence, he'd kill her and escape.

Of course, to earn her trust, he'd have to charm her.

Before, the snow queen had been less than amused at his reluctance. That was why she'd enchanted him in the first place. If he was pliant and agreeable to everything - even her tortures - it was one less thing for her to worry about. So she'd taken away his free will and bespelled him to think he was in love with her. It wasn't too much of a stretch for the mind - she was ethereally beautiful, if cruel. And even with the spell? She still hadn't trusted him not to escape - she'd never given him the freedom to walk her chambers in the past.

But two days ago, she'd taken away the enchantment. And now she was about to invite him to sit at dinner with her.

If he didn't know better, Kai would have sworn that it was an entirely different woman. But the pale brows and white-blonde hair cascading down her back were the same. The dress made of lattices of frost and icicles was the same. The blue eyes that watched him were the same. The deadly command over ice? The same. Only the expressions and mannerisms were different.

It simply had to be a new tactic to get him to let his guard down. Fine then, he'd play her game. Kai gave her his most cajoling smile, but said nothing. If he encouraged her to let him out, she'd suspect something.

She continued to watch him from the other side of the icicle cage, her fingers curling around the thick shafts of ice as she regarded him. It looked as if she were trying to decide if she wanted to trust him.

He held his breath, waiting.

Then she gave a small sigh and the icicles began to crack and vibrate. "Step back," she told him in a soft voice.

"I won't harm you," he told her. Not yet.

This time her mouth twisted into a hint of a smile. "I know. I meant that if you were too close, you might get speared." And the icicles in her hands shattered like glass, the shards tinkling to the floor.

He staggered backward, avoiding the flying ice even as she ignored it, her small hands touching each icicle that made his cage and shattering it with ease. Astonishing. He'd wrapped his hands with the polar bear pelt and tried to break them himself, but they'd proven far too strong.

Strong magic, indeed. And concerning. If she used it, she could destroy him in an instant. He had to be careful.

She brushed aside the shattered icicles. Her efforts had created a small doorway that he could step through. "Sorry about the mess. For some reason, breaking the ice is a lot easier on the magic than just reshaping it."

"I see." He made no move to step forward. "Thank you, Charlotte."

A soft smile touched her face. "You remembered my name."

Kai nodded.

The snow queen stepped aside and gestured for him to walk out of the cell. "Come, then."

He pulled the polar bear hides tight around his body and stepped forward. The air was always frosty when she was around, but he didn't mind the cold lately. It meant that she'd be visiting, and even if he couldn't figure her out, it was better than staring at the ice walls of his prison. Kai stepped out of the cell and immediately felt a bit lighter in spirit. He was halfway to freedom.

"Follow me," she said, and swept past him in a tinkle of ice, her dress shivering with her movements. He studied her as she walked. Even her mannerisms were different, he decided. Before, she'd walked with hard, brisk steps, her movements almost jerky. Now, as she strolled away from him, there was a rolling sway to her hips, and an ease to her steps. She didn't march up the stairs as much as she glided.

Yet it had to be the same woman. Puzzling.

Kai followed her up the stairs, taking his time with each step. Though the floors were patterned with a texture, they were still ice and hard for him to walk on in bare feet. The skins flapped and dragged around him, and not for the first time, he wished for his own clothing.

He followed her into her room and was stunned at the opulence of it. His village was small, their homes modest. Yet this chamber was like something out of fireside tales - it reminded him of a cathedral he'd seen once in a city, all vaulted ceilings and glimmering beauty. At the center of this was a dais shaped like an icy bowl rising from the floor and filled with snow. That must have been her bed. He pictured this creature - so different than the queen of a few days ago - waking from sleep. Her features would be soft, her hair tousled about her head, her limbs languid as she stretched...

And a bolt of arousal struck him. Kai loathed himself for the thought, pulling the furs closer to his body. Nothing but mind games. That was all this was.

Her gasp of surprise caught his attention. Kai turned to her, but she was staring at a small nearby table in surprise. Two place settings had been laid at the table. Her tray of small, colored cubes was accompanied by an equally icy goblet, and across from that was a bowl of soup and a plain ceramic cup.

"Someone was here?" She looked delighted, turning back to him. "Do you think there are servants here? Someone else to talk to?"

"Invisible servants," he told her. "Magical constructs. They anticipate your needs when you voice them. They're not real people. I asked the very same thing when you stole me."

Her hopeful expression dimmed. "Oh."

For some reason, he didn't like that he'd been the one to diminish that excitement on her face. "You told me that you hated having others around."

She looked sad. "I must have had a change of heart. I guess." She sighed and sat down at the table, the icy stool neatly curving to accommodate her. "At least you have something to eat now."

Kai grunted and sat down at the table across from her, careful to layer the polar bear skin over the ice stool left for him. Carefully arranging the furs, he sat and

49

regarded the goblet and bowl left for him. Ceramic. It'd be cool to the touch but wouldn't injure him. He recalled the same cup and bowl from his fuzzy memories of when he'd been enchanted - a sobering reminder that the woman across from him was not meant to be trusted.

No matter how prettily sad she looked.

She glanced at his bowl of milky soup, then at her own brightly colored portion of food. "Would you like some of my dinner, perhaps?"

"No. Not when this has been laid out for me and I know it won't ice over my insides."

"Oh." She stared at one of the colored cubes. "This ice thing is a bit of a pain in the ass, isn't it? Thank God it's only for a month."

"A month?"

"Um, never mind." The snow queen smiled brightly at him. "So tell me more about you."

It was on the tip of his tongue to demand, why should I? But that wouldn't bring her closer to trusting him. If she'd truly lost her memories, this was his time to take advantage of things. "I've told you everything you need to know time and time again," he lied, making his voice as easy as he could. He picked up the ceramic bowl and sipped his dinner. "But you never tell me anything about yourself."

"Oh?" Her blue eyes widened again. Then she frowned. "I'm not sure what I can tell."

A devious non-answer despite her sweet expression. He said nothing, simply drank the nourishing (if tasteless) soup left for him and watched her.

She toyed with one of the icy cubes on her tray, a pink one. "So what did we talk about at dinner if we never talked of our histories?" She lifted it to take a small bite.

He set his bowl down. "We didn't talk much. Mostly I just serviced you with my mouth. It didn't leave a lot of room for talking."

She wheezed, choking on the bite of her dinner. Then she coughed, gulping for air, and covered her mouth. Her face turned a pale, delicate blue - definitely a blush. "I what?"

Despite himself, Kai was fascinated by her reaction. Either she was an incredible actress or she had indeed had something happen to her that caused her personality to revert to some softer, sweeter version of herself. And considering that she was missing all the lies he was dropping? He was starting to become more and more convinced.

This would work well for his plans.

"Shall I show you? Would you like for me to service you again?" He put his bowl down and stood. He wasn't lying about that; he'd had sex with the snow queen. While under the enchantment, he'd have done anything she wanted, and more. He'd been fully aware that he'd hated her even as much as the enchantment forced love into his mind and overrode his reactions. He should be furious at how she'd treated him, but the enchantment had muddled with his memories of those interludes - thankfully - and all he remembered were icy limbs, her wicked, cruel laugh, and a vague sense of resentment in the back of his mind, mixed with pleasure.

But now that she had...changed, he wanted to see how she'd react to his offer.

Her jaw dropped a little, her mouth working, but nothing came out. She recovered a moment later with a small shake of her head, "I,,,no I " Her brow furrowed as she stared at him, at his darker, tanned skin, then back at her own bluish-white skin. He could practically see the question written in her mind. *How does that*

51

work? But she didn't ask, and he was surprised. "No," she said after a moment. "Thank you."

Against his will, his mouth quirked into an amused smile. She was thanking him? "I am here for your pleasure, as you have so often reminded me," he told her. "If you have needs, they are mine to service."

Her eyes narrowed. "Then why did you try to kill me the other day?" She extended one foot out from under the table and he could see the dark-colored welt around her ankle, where he'd grasped it.

She was cleverer than he'd given her credit for. "Madness from the enchantment," he lied quickly. "It confused me."

"I see." Then she shook her head again, squirming slightly in her chair. Then, as if it made her uncomfortable, she bolted up from it and paced across the room. "I don't want you to hurt yourself simply to please me. I'd never ask that."

But she *had* asked that, many, many times. It only convinced him further that somehow her mind had snapped, taking away the evil and leaving behind a stranger. A deadly, albeit fascinating one. And he found himself standing and following her.

"There are many ways I can please you without injury," he told her, surprised at how much he wanted to show this to her. He was fascinated by her wide-eyed reactions to everything. What would she be like in bed? He hated that he even wondered it. He should have been thinking about escape, not about throwing her down onto that snowy bed and ravaging her just to see her gasp. "Shall I show you?"

She trembled, but she wouldn't look at him, as if shy. *Shy.*

He moved to stand behind her. He wanted to reach out and touch her, but didn't. He knew from experience that it would hurt her - and him. Instead, he shrugged off the polar bear skin he had wrapped around his body. "May I touch you?"

"I....I don't know."

He draped the fur over her shoulders. "I'll be gentle." And he rubbed her skin through the fur, gliding a hand along her limbs.

She shivered, biting her lip. Her hands went to the fur that threatened to fall off her shoulders and held it tight. "We shouldn't—"

"Shh," he told her. And his hand skimmed down a fur-covered arm. Her shoulder became exposed as the bear-skin slipped over one arm, and he leaned in and gently blew a soft breath on the exposed skin.

She moaned aloud, her eyes closing.

He froze in place, stunned by her response. Before, she'd never shown any sort of reaction. It had always been coldly clinical to watch her during sex, and he knew that even if he felt pleasure, she got more out of his eagerness for the pain she'd dealt than any caress.

But now? She moaned when all he did was breathe on her.

And his cock became hard as stone in response.

"I wish I could touch you," she whispered.

Just like that, he had a mental image of her, pale hands caressing his cock, that soft, sweet look on her face as her white hair fell about her shoulders. The look of wonder on her face as she explored him. And he was hit by a surge of lust so strong that he staggered. "There are ways," he told her. "You only have to ask."

But she shook her head, looking soft and sad for a moment. "I can't ask that." She shrugged the furs back off her shoulders and held it out to him, turning. "But thank you."

And he noticed that her gaze avoided his naked body.

All right, then. More games. If that was what she wanted, he'd be happy to oblige. He turned back to the table and gestured at the food there. "You might as well finish your meal, My Queen."

The sharp crackle of ice was the only hint that she was using her magic until it was too late. He turned around and barely caught a glimpse of her escaping through one of the icy walls, leaving him alone in her chamber.

She'd fled.

Chapter Four

Charlotte rubbed her arms as she paced the halls of the castle, surrounded by the glassy gleam of ice. Her mind was whirling with everything she'd learned from Kai, and it was too much to take in.

The snow queen was as bad as she'd feared. When she'd seen the ice covering Kai's groin, she'd had a niggle of doubt in her mind that things were bad, but after talking to him? She found out that things were very, very bad, much worse than she'd hoped.

The Queen had been a sadist, and she'd been using Kai for her own pleasure. God, he must hate her. The only person in this icy fortress other than her, and he'd been abused by her. That made her stomach turn. Not only was she stuck on the wrong end of this fairy tale, but she was in the body of a torturer. Suddenly this entire thing had taken an ugly turn.

She gave a self-pitying sniff. She didn't want to be the bad guy.

This was a nightmare. To think that she'd been moderately excited to be the snow queen! To have cool ice powers and a beautiful castle to live in? She didn't want any of this anymore. She wanted to be the heroine. The good guy. Not the one that was enchanting the sexy hero so she could abuse him.

Charlotte...

She froze. Looked around. "Is someone there?"

You know who I am...

The voice didn't sound familiar. With another glance around, Charlotte continued down the hall...and then paused.

She was standing atop the room with the mirror in it.

That creepy, creepy mirror that oozed bad magic.

I can help you...

Swallowing the nervous knot in her throat, she called out, "Um, no thanks! I'm good."

Are you truly? The eerie voice laughed and mocked her. *You seem unsatisfied to me. Perhaps I can help...*

"I'm pretty sure I don't want your help," Charlotte said, stepping out of the hall and adding another layer of ice.

She'd never come down this hall again, if she could help it. She shuddered. Just what was in that mirror, she didn't know, but she didn't like it.

Not one bit.

When Charlotte returned to her room later, she found Kai asleep in her bed, wrapped in the polar bear skins. She was a bit thrown at the sight, then realized that the ice door to his cell was too heavy for normal humans to lift. With a small sigh, she headed to the wall, dragged out enough ice to form an icy couch, and laid down. She pillowed her head on her arm to sleep, wishing she could curl up next to him. He looked so deliciously comfy in her bed, so at ease.

But one touch of her skin would burn him, and she couldn't allow that. Charlotte sighed and closed her eyes, determined to sleep in her new spot. As she drifted off, though, she wondered...

How had the snow queen touched Kai before without hurting him? He'd been covered in ice, but not burned, and he'd admitted they had sex. So what was the key she was missing?

Charlotte avoided Kai that morning. She slipped out through the bedroom walls as soon as she awoke and headed out to do her daily reinforcements on the ice castle battlements. Time was ticking away, and she had to be ready when the heroine showed up to save Kai. The irony of things? Charlotte didn't want to keep him either — she was being forced to by the workings of the fairy tale. The fairy tale in which she should have been the heroine, damn it. Not the bad guy. Irritation made her magic surge, and the wall she was working on sprouted fierce spikes.

"Hard at work, I see?" The cheerful voice interrupted Charlotte's thoughts.

She whirled, surprised to see the small, rotund form of her fairy godmother, Muffin, dressed in a crocheted beach cover up, and a floral one-piece swimsuit, and flip-flops. A wide brimmed yellow hat perched atop her head.

The sight of her startled the heck out of Charlotte. "Oh!" The magic at her fingertips surged and the icy spikes she'd just created shattered into bits.

Muffin raised her eyebrow at Charlotte from over a pair of enormous, oversized sunglasses. "Premature magic ejaculation?"

"Um. Not really? You just surprised me." Though now she was blushing. She shook out her hands, her fingertips re-frosting. "It's so incredibly nice to see you, though!"

"It is?" Muffin blinked in surprise, then gave Charlotte a pleased look. "I don't often get that. Normally I get a 'where the hell have you been, you old bat?' I have to admit I like this much, much better! You're my new favorite."

Charlotte wiped her sweating - okay, more like frosting - brow. "I'm glad I'm someone's favorite, at least."

"Oh dear. That was a sad panda tone of voice if I ever heard one." Muffin pulled a wand out of her oversized beach bag. She waved it at the snow and a bright pink inflated pool lounger appeared. She plopped into it and wiggled, the entire thing squeaking loudly. "Now, tell me all about it, sweetie."

A second inflatable chair appeared next to Muffin's. After a moment of hesitation, Charlotte sat down. "I...I'm just struggling, is all."

"Really? You look like you're doing pretty well to me." Muffin waved a hand at the icy walls of the castle. "I see we've figured out the snow queen powers and we're redecorating in a very angry sort of motif. It's not my usual thing but I can dig it."

Big, fat tears started to well from Charlotte's eyes. "But I don't want to be the snow queen. I was supposed to be the heroine."

Muffin twirled a finger in the air. "Be positive, my dear. When life gives you lemons, make lemonade!"

"I can't make lemonade," Charlotte said in a sad voice. "Just lemon popsicles."

The fairy godmother chuckled. "Good one!"

Charlotte gave her a woebegone look.

"Now, now," Muffin said, reaching over to pat Charlotte's knee. She frowned when her hand stuck to Charlotte's frosty skin, ripped her fingers away, and then blew on the red welts the touch left behind. "I forgot about that. What I was going to tell you, my dear, is that you're still *in* the fairy tale. Things can always get better. As long as you are here, you have a chance to take charge and make changes."

"But I'm the bad guy! Everyone hates me!"

"No, you're the snow queen. You have to do the snow queen stuff. No one says you have to be all bad." She shrugged. "I can't change it. That nitwit intern of mine messed it up, but what's done is done, my dear. Everyone only gets one fairy tale assignment per lifetime. I can't change things. The only thing I can do is check up on you and see how things are going, and maybe offer a little advice here and there."

Charlotte gave a sniff, and then wiped her cheeks. She was being silly. Of course, Muffin was right. At least she had a second chance. "I'm sorry. It's just rough and I'm lonely."

"What about that delicious young man that's been hanging around?"

"Kai?"

"Is he the naked, hot one? Yeah, him." Muffin flicked her fingers. "Go tell him you're lonely. He'll fix that fast, if I'm any judge of these sorts of things."

Charlotte felt her cheeks grow hot. She remembered the hot look in Kai's eyes. *There are ways...* "I don't know that he's offering...friendship, exactly."

Muffin gave a ladylike snort. "That's not what we called it back in my day, either."

How embarrassing. "You know he doesn't really want me, Muffin."

"Of course he doesn't," the fairy godmother said, her expression one of patience. "He thinks you're the snow queen. If he's offering you something, it's because he's trying to gain some leverage."

Charlotte crossed her arms over her icicled chest, a bit annoyed at Muffin's words. "Well, that was blunt."

Muffin straightened her oversized sunglasses. "Trust this old lady, my dear. I've been around the block a few times. Take what that boy's offering, if you're bored. No one's going to judge, least of all not me. Just don't expect more from him than a warm body and a few pretty words."

It was the truth, of course. Charlotte wasn't stupid. Kai had changed directions on her so suddenly that she'd almost had whiplash. The man who'd tackled her and tried to escape her suddenly offering her sex? Of course it was a plot of some kind.

And of course she was a doofus to even consider it. Just a little.

No one's going to judge, least of all, me.

Muffin was right, Charlotte realized. There was no one to judge her, except maybe Kai. If he wanted to use her, couldn't she use him back? Just a little? Take a bit of comfort from whatever he had to offer her, and run with that?

As long as she knew he was using her, and she used him back, what was the harm? She wanted companionship. She was utterly lonely and miserable as the snow queen, and working on the walls only burned through so many hours of the day. What would it hurt to spend more time with Kai and entertain him in his thoughts of escape? It wasn't like she was going to NOT let him free at the end of the month.

Charlotte considered this. As long as both parties got what they wanted, what was the harm?

That night, she decided to test Kai. After a dinner of flavored cubes (and his soup), she gave him a cheery smile. "Want to go for a walk?"

"A...walk?" He gave her a skeptical look, as if expecting a trap.

"Yes, you know, that thing where you put one foot in front of the other?" She mimed feet with her hands. "And you move around? It's quite thrilling, I assure you."

He snorted. "I know what a walk is."

"Oh, good. Then I don't have to explain more of the logistics to you." She teased, brightening. There was none of the bubbling resentment in Kai today, and it made her feel a little better. "Come on, then."

"Where are we going?"

"Just around the castle." She'd been working in the courtyard for hours that day, reinforcing the icy lattice of the walls and trying to figure out if she could somehow make a moat. The problem with a moat, of course, was that it kept freezing over. Still, this place was horribly defended and if she didn't want to lose her head when Kai's girlfriend came calling? She had to do something. So she made the walls thicker and steeper, and they were no longer as pretty but a good deal safer.

It took a lot out of her, though. Every day, she worked for hours in the courtyard, until she was exhausted and her ice powers were puttering out in spurts instead of a steady stream. Work was work, but it was also lonely, and as she'd slaved under the icy sunlight, she'd wished that Kai would be able to join her in the courtyard for company.

So...she was going to test him. They'd take a nice walk around the courtyard, she'd pretend to be distracted, and she'd see if he'd bolt. If he didn't, he could come with her while she worked, and she'd have company and conversation.

If he did...well, then Muffin was wrong and she could never trust Kai.

Gathering her skirts in a crackle of ice, Charlotte headed out of her chambers and through one of the nearby walls. It melted backward as she passed through, and she held the wall open for a few seconds longer to allow Kai to pass through. It was effortless for her now, though she could see from the expression on Kai's face that it was still impressive to him. Chamber after chamber, they passed through, until they descended the icy stairs that led to the front courtyard.

The sun was sinking into the horizon, the skies purple and orange, and the courtyard before her glittered with ice and snow. It was rather pretty if you liked the cold, Charlotte had to admit. There had been an orchard here, once, and the trees rustled and tinkled with the breeze, completely iced over. In the distance, there were rose bushes that were nothing but icy tangles, and a frozen over maze that the former occupant of her body had created. Charlotte hadn't bothered with the maze, since she could just melt the walls with a thought. It sort of made the whole 'maze' thing lose its appeal.

"Well," Charlotte said lightly. "Shall we walk?"

She looked over at Kai and was surprised by the expression on his face. His tan had paled, and there was a look of wonderment and some other emotion she couldn't describe. His eyes gleamed. He looked...upset?

"Oh no. What's wrong?" She reached out to touch his arm, but pulled back before her skin touched his. Damn ice queen business. "Is it all the ice? Because I'm pretty sure that once I'm gone, it'll go back to normal. No need to get upset—"

He shook his head, interrupting her. "This...is the first time I've been outside in months." He tilted his head back and inhaled deeply, as if delighting in the fresh air.

"Oh." Well, didn't that make her feel like an asshole? Or rather, an asshole-by-proxy since she wasn't the original asshole. "I'm glad we're taking a walk, then."

"Yes," Kai said simply, and then fell silent.

Charlotte clasped her hands and began to walk forward, relieved when Kai moved into place at her side. She glanced over at him, wincing at his bare feet and the way he had the furs wrapped around his shoulders. "If you're too cold—"

"I'm fine," he said quickly.

Right. She nodded, and continued strolling, though she tried to consciously thin and warm the ice at her feet so it wouldn't bite at his skin as he stepped.

They walked her enormous courtyard in silence, and as they walked, her thoughts turned to the walls, as always. Here, there was a spot that could be reinforced. There, the ice had made formations that almost looked like steps and she needed to smooth them lest someone use it as a ladder and climb over all her hard work. As they walked, she peeked over at him a few times, but his face was carefully blank.

Well, it was now or never. Steeling herself, Charlotte turned to the jagged ice and approached it, placing her hands on the wall. "Give me a moment. I need to smooth this." She turned her back to him.

And waited.

Her eyes closed, she connected with the ice. She'd been stretching and testing her ice queen powers, since no one had given her a manual. Through testing, she'd eventually figured out that if she concentrated, it was like she could connect to the ice at a molecular level and almost 'see' what was around her. She'd feel any vibrations of movement, striations in the ice that told her something was changing.

If Kai was going to make a break for it, she'd feel every footstep on the ice and know what he was doing without lifting a finger.

This was about trust. And she mentally crossed her fingers and hoped she could trust him. She was so freaking lonely, and captor-and-captive wasn't exactly the most fun relationship. Something had to change.

So she waited. To Kai's eyes, she would appear to be lost in concentration, hands locked against the icy wall. There was not a single sound except the whistle of the chilly wind.

A footstep crunched against the ice.

Charlotte waited. Maybe he was shifting his feet. *Don't do it, Kai. Please don't.*

Another footstep. Then another.

Then, he was running, and her spirits sank. Charlotte pulled her mind out of the ice and whirled around to see Kai sprinting, as fast as he could, for the icy lattice of the portcullis that led to her courtyard. If he could break through that, he could head straight on to the hills.

Or so he thought. She could stop him in an instant. Her heart sank, though. She couldn't trust Kai after all. Not that she was surprised, but she'd hoped...

Oh well. Crossing her arms, Charlotte watched him race across the ice a moment longer, and then knelt to touch her fingertips to the ice-covered ground.

Two hundred feet away, the ice slithered and shifted under Kai's feet, knocking him onto his back. He got to his feet quickly, shaking his head to clear it, and began to race forward again.

But she had him. The ice surged around his feet like quicksand, submerging him up to his calves in ice and locking him in place.

His feral growl of frustration was audible from a distance.

"I thought we were past this," Charlotte called out in annoyance, pacing over to him. "Seriously. An escape? Really? You thought you could get away?"

"I had to try," he snarled at her, twisting his body to give her his best glare as she strolled forward.

Charlotte moved in front of him and kept her arms crossed on her chest, one finger tapping on her forearm. She wanted to yell at him in frustration. She was just so damn disappointed. They couldn't be friends after all, could they? It was all just a big pipe dream.

She suddenly wanted to cry. Was she really going to be stuck, alone and scared, for the next month with no company except a man who wanted nothing more than to flee her presence? She rubbed her stinging eyes, willing the tears away, and then sighed.

Did she blame him? He thought she was the snow queen, and the snow queen was an asshole and a half. Of course he'd run away.

Charlotte dropped to the ground in a crinkle of icy skirts. She was just so very tired of all of this. Being the bad guy was rather taxing on the soul. "Can we talk? Heart to heart?"

Kai glared at her, stiff and angry, his entire body vibrating with rage.

She threw her hands up. "Just talk, okay? Nothing more. No tricks. Just talk."

He relaxed a bit, but then added, "I can't feel my feet."

"Oh. Oops." Charlotte touched the ground, releasing the ice covering him to his calves. He danced out of its grasp, stomping his bare feet on the ground, and then set the fur on the ice, crossing his legs and rubbing his toes to bring warmth back into them.

And he gave her another grouchy glare.

"Sorry about that," she told him. "I had to see if you were going to run. Looks like I was right."

"Like I said, I had to try."

"I know. And I don't blame you. I really don't. I just..." she sighed heavily. "Can we be friends? Truce? I'm here for the next month and I'd really like it if we could stop hating each other."

He gave her another wary look. "You're not going to punish me?"

"Why should I?"

"You have always punished me severely for escape attempts in the past." He watched her closely. "The last time, you put the mirror flecks in my eyes to enchant me into falling in love with you."

She chewed on her lip, thinking. She remembered the mirror flecks and how they'd made him into some sort of lovesick zombie. "Nah, I'm good. Like I said, I don't blame you for trying. I'm just disappointed, is all."

Kai stared at her for so long that her nape began to prickle, uncomfortable. Then, he leaned forward, his voice low as his dark eyes regarded her. "Who are you, really?"

Charlotte clasped her hands nervously. "I'm the Snow Queen."

"No," he said flatly. "You are not. You wear her form, but you are not her."

She couldn't stop herself from wringing her hands in worry. If Muffin knew that he'd guessed the truth, would she be in trouble? She'd had to promise not to discuss it, or else everything would be ruined. "Yes, I am," she said emphatically, and gave a little nod.

"You're different. You don't remember anything from before. You don't touch me the way you used to. And you want to be...friends." He said the last word flatly. "You are not the same woman."

"Hssst!" Charlotte shushed him, waving her hands and glancing around anxiously in case the fairy godmother was nearby, listening. "Ixnay on that whole line of thinking, okay?"

"Tell me the truth," he demanded.

She clenched her fists. "Look, Kai, I wish I could, but I can't, okay? I just can't. Please trust me." Frustrated tears threatened again. "I don't like this any more than you do."

"Then tell me who you are!"

"I'm the goddamn Snow Queen!" Charlotte jerked to her feet. "You may not believe me, but it's true. You think I'm doing all this ice bullshit for funsies? It's who I have to be. And I'm going to protect my ass as best as I can so I can win this stupid task I'm being shoved through."

His dark eyes glared at her, as hard as the line of his mouth. After a moment, he asked, "You mentioned a month. A month and something happens. And you're changing things. You're changing all of this into a fortress." He gestured at the no-longer pretty and dainty ice walls. "Why?"

She snapped her mouth shut, mentally cursing. She'd said too much. He'd caught her little slip of the tongue and now she was going to be in trouble for sure. But when no fairy godmother struck her down, she supposed that she hadn't broken the rules...

Yet.

Charlotte rubbed her forehead. "I can't say."

"What happens at the end of the month?"

She glared at him. "I still can't say."

"Are you going to tell me anything?"

"I honestly don't think that I can. Not without getting both of us into trouble."

Kai snorted at that, and rubbed his foot a little harder, forcing circulation back into his chilled flesh.

"You make it sound as if you have someone you answer to."

She pressed her lips together, still silent.

"Do not tell me, then," he said. "I will harbor my own suspicions. But tell me this: what will happen to me at the end of the month?"

"If it's up to me?"

"Yes."

"I'll let you go. You can go home."

He looked surprised. "You'd just let me leave?"

"That's right."

His brows furrowed. "You make it sound as if I'm a guest instead of your prisoner."

She wanted to tell him that none of this was her idea, but she forced herself to press her lips closed, keeping her secrets.

"Very well, then," Kai said, wiggling his toes. He gave her a scrutinizing look. "You will keep me as a companion for this month, and then you will let me go. Why?"

She shrugged. "Maybe I needed a friend."

He stared at her for so long that her cheeks felt heated with a flush. "A friend," he said flatly.

Now she felt stupid. "Whatever you may think of me, it's true. All *I* want from you is a friend."

"I see." He thought for a moment, and then gestured at the furs he sat on. "If we are to be friends, I want clothing. And boots."

"If I knew how to get those, you'd have them already." She gave him a wry smile. "I'm not exactly sure who is in charge of shopping around here."

"You have servants, remember?"

Right, so she did. "I'll put them right on that." Just as soon as she figured out how.

When Kai went to bed that night in the snow queen's chambers, his mind was troubled. Well, no, that wasn't quite right. His mind was always troubled when it came to her, but now he was simply confused.

She wasn't the same person as before.

Oh, she'd danced around the subject and given him vague answers, but what she hadn't admitted to had told him plenty. *Look, Kai, I wish I could, but I can't, okay? I just can't. Please trust me. I don't like this any more than you do.*

She — Charlotte, he had to think of her as Charlotte - made it sound like she was not here of her own choosing. More games? He didn't know. But when she'd said she wanted a friend...he'd believed her.

Maybe she'd be true to her word and release him at the end of the month, like she promised. He considered her words. *Maybe I wanted a friend.*

Very well, then. He'd give her a friend. Bees flock to honey because it is sweet, the old saying went. He'd get further with her if it seemed like he was playing along with whatever her new game was. If it was a game at all. He hadn't missed the sheer disappointment on her face when she'd caught him escaping, but she looked sincere when she said she hadn't blamed him.

Kai didn't know what to make of her.

Even now, he lay alone in her bed, wrapped in the blankets. He held his breath, listening to the stillness. Tonight, as every night, he heard the muffled sound of weeping.

So she was a different woman, and she cried every night. And she couldn't tell him anything about who she was or why she was wearing the same face as the snow queen.

One thing was certain, though; she was no happier to be here than he was.

Chapter Five

Something stirred Kai out of sleep. He remained still, his breathing even, as he assessed the situation. His fingers twitched, desperate for his hunting knife, but the snow queen had shattered it moments before she'd captured him.

His ears pricked as he caught the low sound of murmuring voices. Was that Charlotte? Who was she talking to? Her servants? But...why in the middle of the night?

Carefully, he sat up in the icy nest, wrapping the furs around his body. The low sound of voices continued, so he tucked a smaller fur around his hips, forming a kilt, and tiptoed through the room, looking for the sound of the voices.

He went down another hallway before the voices started again.

"But, I don't want to be the snow queen," he heard Charlotte saying. "I'm just a normal woman. I'm not the bad guy!"

"You're a whiner," a high, nasally voice said emphatically.

"Now, now, Fifi," said another voice. "Let's be nice to our clients, all right? What she meant to say, Charlotte,

71

was that when life gives you lemons, you make lemonade."

"You keep saying that, and I'm tired of hearing it! There's no lemonade to be made here! You've put me in an impossible situation! Do you understand that if I win this, I screw over Kai and his girlfriend and everyone in the village? They can't live in all this ice! Nothing grows! I'm destroying the crops and their livelihoods simply by being here."

"Then lose," the kind voice said. "If you value the lives of strangers more than your own, lose and this won't be a problem."

"But you told me if I lose this challenge, I'll be stuck between worlds forever, right?"

"Well, yes, that's right."

"Then I can't lose," Charlotte's voice rose to a panicked level. A sob escaped her throat. "What am I supposed to do?"

"Well, crying about it won't help," came the nasal voice again.

"Fifi," the other one warned.

"She's whining," the nasal one continued. "I thought you said she'd be happy for a second chance?"

"Well, most of them are."

"Not this one! All we hear is 'waaah, I'm so sad that I have to be the bad guy. It's so awful that I have all these magic powers and get to live in an ice castle. Oh, my life is sooo terrible'."

"You suck," Charlotte said in a tear-choked voice. "It's your fault I'm here. I'm supposed to be the other girl! The one that Kai likes! Not his enemy! I wish you hadn't messed everything up!"

"Wish in one hand, shit in the other, see which one—
"

"FIFI!"

The quarreling voices fell silent.

What in all the heavens was going on? Who was the snow queen arguing with? Why did she keep saying that this wasn't supposed to be her?

"Please," Charlotte said after a long moment. "I just want to go home."

"I've told you before," the authoritative voice said. "You cannot go home. You cannot be transferred. You are, for all intents and purposes, an evil queen. You're stuck, so why not have fun with it? You're evil! Cut loose! Go wild! This is your second chance to cram in everything you never got to do before!"

"You're my fairy godmother!" He heard Charlotte cry. "I thought you were supposed to help me!"

"I am helping you! Look, this is me playing the world's smallest violin at poor you, stuck with a second chance at life as a magical queen."

"Ugh!" Footsteps slammed on the ice, and Kai barely had time to slide against one glittering wall before Charlotte swept out of the room in a puff of frost, swiping at her eyes. She stormed away, heading for her apartments, and Kai was pretty sure he heard the sound of weeping.

He wanted to go after her. For some reason, her crying tore at him. Maybe it was because he'd never heard her cry until she'd changed? Or maybe it was that he was sensing she was just as trapped as he was. Who had she been talking to?

Curiosity won out, and Kai cracked open the ice-lattice door to the room that Charlotte had left behind.

The room was empty. He frowned, stepping inside and looking around. No one was there. He ran his fingers along every wall surface, looking for a door he might have missed, but there was nothing.

Odd.

Maybe he'd overheard a conversation with her invisible servants. He glanced around, wondering if someone lurked silently in the corners. But there was no one, and nothing to see. It was all so strange.

When he returned to her room, Kai was surprised to see that her eyes were red and swollen, and her nose looked like a red berry. She'd been crying, and was obviously still upset. She had one of the fur satchels and was tossing cubes into it, along with anything else in arm's reach.

"Who were you talking to?" he asked.

"I can't say," she said with a sniff.

He'd expected that answer. It still irritated him to hear it. She shared nothing with him. Not that he expected otherwise – she was his captor. Still, she kept trying to convince him that she was different...and then did the same sort of thing that made it difficult for him to trust.

He watched her for a minute more. "What are you doing, then?"

"Packing," she said in a watery voice. She wiped her eyes and shook the ice off of her fingers. "I'm taking a vacation."

"What about me?"

"You'll be fine here in the ice keep," she said in a dull voice. "I've reinforced the doors. You won't be able to get out, but no one will be able to get in, either."

"I'll make a fire and burn a hole through," he threatened. Why did he care if she left him? Why did it make him so angry?

"No, you won't. It's enchanted ice."

"Enchanted how?"

"Um. Enchanted not to burn."

He'd never heard of such a thing. "I don't believe you."

She flushed. "I don't care if you believe me or not. It's true. You're stuck here. And I'll be...back soon. Ish." Her face crumpled and she wiped more tears from her eyes.

For some reason, her tears tore at him. He felt helpless to assist her. In her own way, she'd been kind to him, and he could do nothing in return. "And who will bring me food while you're gone?"

She stilled, blinking.

Ahah. He'd found something she had not considered. "Your servants only respond to you. Who will bring me water and soup when you are gone? Or do you care if I starve? Is this another one of your tortures?"

He knew she hated it when he threw out the 'torture' word.

Sure enough, her jaw set in a mulish line. "I'm not torturing you."

"I seem to recall ice in unpleasant places that tells me otherwise."

Her face flushed again, rather prettily. "That's not fair."

"Is it not? What about this is fair?"

She threw her bag down, now angry at him. "I didn't choose this!"

"Nor did I."

Her mouth firmed again.

"If you're leaving, take me with you," he said, though he wasn't sure why. She just seemed so desperately alone and unhappy. "You can keep an eye on your prisoner and still get away."

She hesitated, and then began to stuff the furs in the bag. "You'll need furs. You can't go naked."

"I'll get them," he said easily.

He didn't know why, but he felt like he'd won a battle. "Where are we going?"

"Anywhere but here," she said, a grim look on her pretty face. "I'm not staying here to wait for the end."

"The end?"

She turned and glanced around the room, then looked at him. "Someone's coming here and I doubt they're leaving without my head on a pike."

"I'm sick to death of this place."

She wasn't the only one. "We can go south, to my people."

Charlotte gave him a pointed look. "Yeah, right."

He found himself smiling. "I had to ask."

Her tears dried a little, and her mouth turned up, just slightly, at the corners. "I suppose you did."

"So...where are we going?"

She shrugged. "There's a mountain in the distance. I thought I'd see what was on the other side."

"Walking?"

She thought for a moment, and then got a mischievous look on her face. "Not walking..."

From atop the back of her polar bear, Charlotte stared over the cliff. "Okay, so apparently there is no other side of this mountain."

Behind her rode Kai, his hands on her icy waist. "This is probably why no one lives on the mountain," he said with amusement. "My people never come here."

That struck her as odd. "Really? Even when I wasn't here?"

"It is a long climb and my people travel by foot." His long black hair fluttered near her face as the wind picked up. "We've had to range further and further for food due to the cold, but never up the mountain. As you can see, there is not much to commend this side."

He had a point. Charlotte pushed her hair back behind an ear and studied the world laid out below them. Their polar bear (she'd asked her invisible servants for a mount and this was what had showed up) waited patiently on a narrow, snowy ledge. Far below, the craggy granite of the mountain seemed to sheer off, leading to white-capped waves and floating glaciers hundreds of feet below. If she squinted, she could make out dozens of dark, lounging forms below. Walruses, or seals, perhaps. The wind was high, whipping her hair about no matter how much she tried to tie it back, and seagulls cried out in the distance. It was all very beautiful.

Not super useful, but beautiful. "Do your people fish?"

"They do. Why?"

She pointed below, at a seal flopping across the ice. "They're obviously eating something. My guess is that there's some good fishing below."

"Yes, so I will just tell my starving people that if they will only cross an icy mountain and then scale a cliff, there is fishing to be had. I will carry that message home as soon as you let me go." His voice was full of harsh sarcasm.

She winced. "Okay, okay, good point. I was just trying to think of a way to make everyone happy."

"You could send me home."

They'd had this argument before. "I will in about two weeks."

He grunted amicably.

For some reason, their arguments about sending him home had lost a lot of their bite. Even though they'd ridden together today into the wild, he'd never once attempted to leave her side or overpower her. In fact, it had almost seemed as if both of them were enjoying the afternoon out in the wild.

Either that, or they were enjoying being together. She was, but she was starved for company. She might have been assuming that he was enjoying himself as much as she was. But there was no animosity between them. And...she really liked it.

Charlotte gazed down at the glacier-peppered waters, at the seals basking in the sun on the sand below the cliff. All that food, and too remote for his starving people to get to. They'd have to pass her icy domain, up the mountain, and then, as Kai had said, find a way down the cliff.

And she was no help. She was the bad guy. She sighed. "It's a shame I'm not the crop princess instead of the snow queen."

He snorted. "You'd have to pry me from your side if that were true."

And wouldn't that be a lovely problem to have? Charlotte gazed wistfully down at the blue waters below. If she had Kai's help, she wouldn't be running away from her ice castle so his avenging girlfriend wouldn't come and kill her. If only Kai was on her side. She thought for a moment, then asked, "What happens if I win?"

"What do you mean?" Kai's hands shifted on her waist. She could have sworn she felt his hands give a bit of a comforting squeeze, but perhaps she'd imagined it. He often had to adjust his hands - his fox-skin gloves tended to stick to her icy clothing if he didn't shift or move about every so often.

"Your people will come after you in two weeks. It's been foretold." Well, if a fairy tale was considered a divination of the future. "When they do, they'll either win or I'll win. What happens if I win, do you suppose?"

"Unending winter," Kai said softly. "Endless cold. You'll be the queen of a dead land. No one will live here or be able to survive here."

She gazed down at the seals below. They seemed happy and well-fed enough. But she knew what Kai meant - there'd be no people. There'd be nothing for them to eat, no crops to harvest. She'd be alone, a queen of nothing but ice. But...people could survive in cold, if they knew how. Entire Native populations lived in icy Alaska and Canada and they seemed to cope just fine. But Kai's people weren't prepared for that sort of lifestyle, and she couldn't blame them.

Charlotte didn't know what to do. Either she screwed over an entire kingdom, or she destroyed herself. Logic told her to be self-sacrificing and to give herself up for the good of the many, but this wasn't just death and then moving on to the Afterlife. This was *no* Afterlife. She'd just cease to exist, full stop.

And that was completely terrifying.

"I hate being the bad guy," she said abruptly. "Hate it, hate it, hate it! I don't want to be evil!"

"So don't," Kai said.

She sighed and slid off the side of the polar bear. She couldn't sit still; she was too agitated. "You don't understand. I'm the snow queen—"

"You have a lot of magic," he agreed. "A lot of power. If you don't want to be evil, then do something about it."

He made it sound so simple. "Like what?"

"You're the one with the ice powers. If you can come up with unique ways to build your castle, unique ways to travel up the mountain, and unique ways to torture me, why can you not think of ways to do something good with your powers?"

She blinked. Thought for a moment. Blinked some more. Why...had it never occurred to her that she could do something other than evil? She'd simply heard the label 'evil queen' and assumed the worst. Fifi had put her in the wrong person, and she'd just gone along with it. She'd accepted the fact that she was 'bad' and whined instead of doing something about it. She'd moped instead of taking action.

Who said she had to *be* the bad guy? She could do whatever she wanted with these powers. If she could feed

Kai, maybe she could feed everyone. She just had to figure out how. If she could make ice cubes that were food appear out of midair - and a nourishing soup for Kai as her captive...why couldn't she do more?

Who said she couldn't? Muffin and Fifi weren't here to stop her. So the fairy tale got a bit more off the rails? So what?

"Oh my God," she said softly, her hand going to her breast. She could feel her heart pounding with excitement all the way through her skin and her icy bodice.

"What?" Kai slid off the side of the polar bear and approached her, his bundled furs sweeping through the snowy path. He regarded her cautiously. "What is it?"

"I have...choices." A laugh bubbled up in her throat, and for a moment, she felt so light and free that she wanted to dance. She twirled in a circle, her gown tinkling with the movement. "Oh my God, I have *choices!*"

"Careful," Kai said, putting out a warning hand and stopping closer to her. "You're near the edge and I don't want you to slip and fall."

She grabbed his arms and laughed, spinning him around with her. "I'll just make ice to break our fall. It doesn't matter! We're going to fix things, Kai!"

"We are?" he asked, amused. His long, black hair ruffled about as they spun in a slow circle, and she felt his gloves go back to her waist again, pulling her closer to him.

"You're the best, you know that?" she said, still giddy with excitement. Impulsively, she grabbed him and hugged him close, then immediately pulled away. "Oh, I'm not touching you, am I?" She didn't want to hurt him.

But the look on Kai's face was odd. He was watching her, that intense expression on his face. And Charlotte froze in place, her arms still around him, intensely aware of his scorching body heat and just how close their mouths were.

The atmosphere felt charged. Not with magic, like it normally did when she drew her power around her. With something entirely different. Her breathing became quick, excited, but she didn't move away. She didn't want to pull out of his embrace. She didn't want him to stop looking at her with that heated, sleepy expression of lust.

Because, oh heavens, she loved that look on his face.

Slowly, Kai raised a mittened hand and caressed her cheek, tracing the lines of her face. She longed to lean into his touch, to press her mouth to his fingers, but it was only the soft fur of the glove and not his hot skin.

And she wanted more than just this. "Kai," she said softly.

"I know," he murmured, tracing his gloved fingers along one of her eyebrows and then caressing her cheek again. "I'm being careful. I just wanted to touch you."

"You did?"

"It's impossibly strange to me, but you're not the same woman you were. I don't know how or why it's changed, but...I'm drawn to the new you. I can't get enough of you. Whenever you leave, I can't stop thinking about you." His mouth drew in a reluctant smile. "I keep checking my eyes to see if the mirrors have somehow returned, but there's nothing. I'm as clear of mind as I ever was...and yet I can't stop thinking about what it'd be like to put my mouth on you. *This* you."

Her breath caught in her throat. "I wish I could touch you. Skin to skin. I miss that kind of touch."

"There are things we can do, if you'll let me," Kai told her softly. "If you're willing to let me touch you how I wish to."

A shiver rippled through her body as her imagination went wild.

81

"Will you let me?" Kai asked, dragging that soft, ticklish glove down the column of her neck and grazing it across her collar bones.

"Yes," Charlotte breathed. It wasn't even something she had to think about. She wanted his touch. She wanted him. She craved it. "As long as it won't hurt you."

"It shall be exquisite torture, but I don't mind that," he said, and released her from his grip. "Tell your bear we want to return to the castle."

"We do?" She was a little disappointed at the thought. "Why?"

His smile grew broader. "Because there's no need to run. We'll figure things out together. And because you're safest there."

She was surprised he was worried about her safety - surprised, and touched. Charlotte smiled and gave Kai a shy look. "Let's go back, then."

By the time they returned to the Fortress of Solitude (as she was starting to think of it - maybe it was time to pull out some Superman decorating motif), night had fallen and stars twinkled in the clear skies above. The air was a crisp, lovely cold that felt wonderful on her skin, though she suspected it was brutally cold if Kai's occasional shiver gave her any indication. Charlotte felt guilty that he couldn't huddle against her for warmth - she was probably colder than anything else in the area.

The bear paused outside of the gate she'd made, waiting. Charlotte closed her eyes and summoned her magic, like sucking in a breath. Then, she blasted it out with a single thought, and opened her eyes to watch the gate melt away. The bear lumbered forward again, and the moment they crossed the threshold, she repeated the burst of magic, giving herself a migraine. Her power was sapped at the moment, and she slumped on the bear's back.

"Charlotte?" Kai asked, and a mitten touched her shoulder. "Are you well?"

"Just give me a moment to recover," she said softly. "It took a lot out of me." Normally she didn't expel quite so much force in such a short period of time. Her head throbbed, reminding her that she was pushing herself too hard. She slid off the side of the bear and nearly collapsed on the ground, her knees giving out. Perhaps she'd pushed herself harder than she meant to this time.

To her surprise, a warm arm went over her shoulders and another behind her knees, and then she was being hauled into the air and cradled against a broad chest. "I've got you," Kai told her.

"I can walk," she protested weakly. "Really." But oh, it was nice to be tucked against him and carried. She'd never been carried before. Actually, she'd never had anyone take care of her before. It was…refreshing, really. To be able to relax for a moment and let down her guard? It was…nice.

When he snorted a protest, she didn't complain, just tucked her hands against his furs and let him carry her inside, through the winding corridors of the ice palace and into her palatial bedroom. There was her icy nest, just as she'd left it, and Kai gently laid her down inside.

"Rest," he told her. "Your bear can take care of itself. I can take care of myself. But all of this," he said, gesturing at the palace, "needs you to be well. Understand?"

She nodded up at him, resisting the urge to rub her throbbing forehead. "Maybe I'll close my eyes for just a minute."

"Do that," he said sternly, peeling off his cape and laying it over her as a blanket. As if she needed a blanket.

Still, she snuggled underneath it, the scent of Kai in her nostrils, and went to sleep.

Chapter Six

Next to him, Charlotte cried out.

Kai bolted awake and sat up, rubbing his eyes. The chamber was frosty, his breath puffing, and he tugged the blankets higher over their bodies. He'd gone to sleep clothed in his furs so he could curl up next to her while she slept.

There was no reason to do so, but he'd wanted to. He liked touching her and being near her, just like how he couldn't seem to get enough of looking at her. And this was nothing like the mirror spell from before, when he'd felt drugged and doped out of his mind, unable to process anything but the commands she'd given him. He was in full control of his facilities...and still obsessed with this sweeter, gentler version of the snow queen who went by the name of Charlotte and talked to people that he couldn't see.

The snow queen that was just as trapped here as he was. Kai gazed down at Charlotte's sleeping face, wondering at her secrets.

Even now, as he studied her, she tossed and turned, shaking her head. Her eyelids fluttered in her sleep. "No..." she murmured, a distressed sound. "Don't...come back!" When she shook her head again, tiny crystalized tears sprinkled the bedding.

A nightmare. Kai adjusted one of his mittens, tightening the laces to ensure it stayed on. Then, he gave in to the urge to touch her, stroking her cheek with the backs of his gloved fingers. "Charlotte. Awaken, Charlotte. You're having a bad dream."

She flinched, and then her eyes flew open, and her lashes fluttered as her blue eyes struggled to focus in the dim light. "K-k-kai?"

"It's me," he said softly. "You're safe."

Her breasts heaved, her ice bodice creaking with each lungful of air she sucked in. "God. Oh God. That was the worst dream ever. I..." she looked at him and then clamped her mouth shut. "I'm okay, really. Thank you."

He didn't like that she'd pulled back, a wary look on her face. "What were you dreaming about?"

"Nothing."

"It's not nothing," he argued. "You were shaking and crying What was it?" It was obvious to him that the dream had frightened her...and just as obvious that she didn't want to share it with him. That made him feel helpless. He wanted to help her. To comfort her. And he couldn't if she pursed her lips and looked away, like she was now.

So he distracted her again, running the soft fur of his mitten along her jaw again. "Charlotte," he coaxed. "Tell me."

She shook her head again. "It's nothing, Kai. Really."

"Was it about the prophecy you mentioned?" He asked, brushing the mitten across her gleaming brow. He could have stopped touching her at any time, truly. He just...didn't want to. She was snuggled in bed next to him, looking soft and oh-so vulnerable, and he couldn't help it. He had to caress her, even if it was through this gods-blighted mitten of his. He longed to touch her skin, to touch her like a man touched his lover, but they had to be so very careful at all times.

It was frustrating.

"I'm fine," she said softly. "Really."

He doubted that very much. Even now, she seemed to be trembling quietly under the thick furs. He knew she couldn't shiver with cold, so it had to be fear. Kai kept touching her, this time brushing a lock of hair from her brow and smoothing his glove down to her bared shoulder. "Something tells me that you're as terrible a liar as you are an evil queen."

Her mouth quirked sadly at that, but she shifted in the blankets and raised an arm over her head, resting it on one of the pillows tucked beneath her head. "Thank you for waking me, Kai." Her sleepy, soft gaze moved over him restlessly. "Why are you still in your furs?"

So I could press against you while you slept, he wanted to tell her. But he kept silent. If she was going to keep her secrets, he'd keep his own, too. Instead, he studied her. With her arm over her head, her breasts had risen higher, nearly pushing out of her icy bodice. If she moved just a little more, he'd see a glimpse of nipple. Were they pert and tiny under that bodice, begging for his touch?

Gods, he wanted to touch her.

As if sensing his thoughts, Charlotte licked her lips. "Kai?" Her voice was soft. "Talk to me. I can't stand the silence."

"You're beautiful." His fingers traced one white shoulder, and he wished he could touch her skin without the glove. Without barriers.

"I like it when you touch me," she told him in a quiet, achingly sweet voice. "I've missed being touched so badly. I wish we could kiss."

"We can't," he murmured, and leaned in. His long, black hair fell over his shoulder and brushed against her creamy skin, and she shivered in response. "But I can do things to pleasure you, if you'll let me."

She licked her lips, her eyes growing bright with interest. "Only if I can do the same to you."

"I am yours."

Her brow furrowed and anger flashed across her face. "No," she said, her hand clasping his through the glove and stopping his leisurely exploration of her. "You're not mine. You belong to you and no one else. Remember that, Kai. All right? Whatever, whoever I was before? I don't own you."

You may not own me, but you've enslaved me all the same, he thought again, but didn't disagree with her. Instead, when she lifted her hand from his, he brushed down one bared arm. "Can I touch you?"

"Of course."

"All of you?"

She sucked in a soft breath, and then gave a small wriggle on the bed. Now both arms were above her head and she closed her eyes. As she did, her icy clothing seemed to shimmer and melt into her skin. A moment later, it all disappeared as if it had never been, and she was soft and naked and bare next to him.

Kai gazed down at her utter perfection. Her breasts were perfect round globes, her nipples the palest blue he'd ever seen, so pale they almost blended with the rest of her skin. The tips were small and tight, pebbled with arousal. Her stomach was slightly curved and her hips flared out to long, tapered legs and tiny feet.

And covering her sex was silky white floss that matched her hair.

He'd never seen her naked with his senses about him. Flashes of memory told him that he'd possibly seen her naked when he was ensorcelled by the mirror, but the memories belonging to that time had disappeared as soon as the spell had. She looked pale and fragile next to him, but the look on her face was one of anticipation and desire, and it made his cock harden with need.

"I'm going to touch you now," he told her, and brushed one of the gloves down the length of a pale arm, readying her for more.

She nodded, anticipation making her cheeks flush an attractive hint of icy blue. There was no fear in her eyes, only excitement, and that aroused him even more. He'd never met a woman quite like her. Perhaps Gerda, who had an enthusiastic lust for life, but he thought of Gerda as a little sister more than a lover.

His covered hand swept back up her arm, and then brushed across her chest, gliding down between the twin mounds of her breasts. He watched as her breathing increased, her breasts rising with excitement as his touch grew bolder. "Is your skin as soft as I imagine it is?" he asked her.

She licked her lips again, and they gleamed icy cool. "I think so."

"I'd love to touch it and find out for myself."

She shivered, her nipples thrusting up toward him, taunting him. "You can't touch me for long, not with bare skin. You need some sort of barrier or we'll both burn."

At this moment, he'd have burned with her if she'd asked. But the thought of hurting her made him sweep the glove over her skin again, and then brush the soft fur of it over one nipple.

Charlotte gasped and arched against his hand, a silent plea for more.

He'd give her more. He'd give her everything he could. His cock was a needing ache in his own now-tight loincloth, but he'd ignore it to pleasure her. His own would come later, at the sight of her when she came from his touch.

Because he definitely planned on making her come.

"I wish my fingers were playing with this nipple," he said, caressing it through the mitten and admiring as she moaned and arched in response. "I'd tease it with my fingers and pluck at it until it was aching for more. Then I'd put my mouth on it and lick and suck at it until you were wild with need."

She bit her lip and moaned a sound that resembled his name. Her hands fluttered, went to the mitten, and then pressed it hard against her breast.

Gods, now his cock throbbed like an aching tooth. He rubbed his fingers over the tip of her breast, rolling her nipple, and then pinched it.

Charlotte gasped, her hips bucking in response.

He wanted to fill her, to push between those thighs and spread them wide, then plow into her and claim her as his own. The need to take her rattled him, made his own breath hitch as he struggled for control. The thick fur protected him from the cold of her body, but it was maddening to not be able to touch her. He wanted to rip the glove off and shove two fingers deep inside the sweet well between her legs, thrusting like his cock wanted to thrust deep inside her—

"We need a barrier," he said suddenly, pulling his hand away and beginning to strip off the mitten. "I have an idea."

"What?" she asked, sitting upright. She was panting and flushed, and looked delectable in her arousal. Gods, he wanted to touch her. For a moment, the glorious sight of her with her breasts heaving and her pale hair tumbling about her shoulders distracted him, and he forced his thoughts back in the right direction.

Kai stripped off the glove and flexed his fingers in the chilly air. He'd test on his hands, first, and if that worked, perhaps they'd progress to...other things. He paired his first two fingers together and extended them toward her. "Ice my fingers."

"Ice them?" She looked confused, and then the confusion gave way to a sultry little gasp. "What are you going to do with them?"

"I'm going to fuck you with them," he said, voice husky with need.

"Won't I...won't that hurt you?" She looked concerned.

"It won't," he lied. Truth was, he didn't know. But there was only one way to find out. He studied her and then decided to give in to a visual fantasy he'd had for a while. "Open your mouth. I want to feed them to you. Lick them and the ice will coat my fingers."

She moaned softly but leaned forward, lips parted, awaiting him.

Saying a quick prayer to the gods that he wouldn't damage himself irreparably, he set his fingers against her lips and then pushed them slowly in. And ah, gods have mercy, the look of her sweet mouth taking him in was almost enough to override the sharp flash of pain that shot up his arm. His skin prickled, but he remained in place, because she was moaning with abject pleasure.

And gods, he loved seeing that.

Slowly, achingly, he pulled his fingers out of her sweet mouth. They were numb with cold, sharp, flashing tingles moving through his skin. A thin layer of ice coated them, just like he'd suspected. He pushed them between her lips again. "Suck."

She did, and the tingles increased slightly, but there wasn't that jolt of pain like before. She made a little mewling sound when he pulled his fingers away from her wet - gods, it was wet and plump and he wanted to fuck it - mouth.

"Are you hurting?" she asked softly, her eyes dazed with lust.

91

"No," he said. "It's nothing. Only a little cold." He intended on getting her off before he admitted to any pain. With his ice-stiffened fingers, he trailed them down her chest, stopping to circle a nipple.

Charlotte moaned, her hips rising again. "Please, Kai."

"I know," he murmured. "Be patient. I'll give you pleasure."

He couldn't feel his fingers any longer, and really, that was the worst of it. He wanted to feel her. Wanted to feel her flesh under him. But if this was going to work, he was going to have to be fast. Kai trailed his fingers lower down her belly, dipping at her navel, and then slid his iced fingers to the mound of her pussy and began to rub back and forth between her juices.

Immediately, the ice began to build on his fingers, thickening at the tip from her wetness. "You're very wet, aren't you?" It was odd to see that she was wet despite the chill of her body, but it formed ice as quickly as it left contact with her skin.

"Oh God, I need you, Kai," she cried, reaching for him and then withdrawing before she could touch him. Her hands fluttered, as if she didn't know where to put them, and then went behind her head to her pillow and clung there. Her legs fell open, inviting him to do more.

He slid his fingers through her wetness, searching for her clitoris. It was hard to tell considering he couldn't spread her lips wide to see it, and he couldn't feel in his fingers to know if he was touching it. So he watched her reactions instead. He knew he hit the spot when her back arched and her mouth went wide, as if screaming, but no sound came out.

There, he rubbed over and over again.

Her head thrashed on the pillow, her moans increasing. "Kai," she panted. "Oh God, Kai, please. I'm so close."

"I've got you," he told her, even though it was foolish to say so. He didn't have her. He couldn't even touch her, really. His fingers would probably get frostbite if this continued much longer, and the numbness and prickles were spreading to the rest of his hand and up his arm, but he wanted to see her come.

Gods above, he wanted to see that.

He pulled his frozen fingers away from her pussy and she whimpered in response. "Spread your legs wider," he commanded, and was pleased when she did. He wanted to make her come, just from his touch. He needed to see that to appease the ache in his own body. He pushed his fingers into the well of her pussy, and then sank them deep inside her, stroking her with them as if they were his cock.

Her legs clenched and she threw her head back, the cords in her neck growing tight as she gasped again. "Oh God, I'm so close, Kai!"

She needed more. He began to push his fingers in and out of her, fucking her like he desperately wanted to with his cock. She continued to squirm under him, but it was clear that no matter how many times he thrust into her with his fingers, she needed a bit more to push her over.

An idea struck him, and he leaned in. "Spread your pussy for me, Charlotte."

She trembled, trembled all over even as he thrust harder and faster into her core. But she did, reaching for her wet, gleaming folds. Her fingers delicately spread her petals like a flower, exposing her clit that was surely aching like his cock was. Thrusting hard with his fingers, he leaned closer to that delicate spot and ever so gently breathed a huff of warm air on it.

Charlotte squealed, and her legs clenched, the muscles jerking as he watched. "Kai," she cried out. He did it again, his breath as gentle and hot as he could make it, just barely a puff against her sensitive skin, even as he plunged his fingers deep inside her.

She cried out then, coming with force. The tendons in her neck stood out again and she gasped and trembled. A rush of wetness coated his fingers and ice formed on the rest of his hand. Another sharp pain ripped through him and he pulled out of her, though he couldn't help but lick the ice coating his fingers. Gods, it tasted like her, sweet and musky all at once. "Melt the ice for me, sweet Charlotte."

She writhed on the bed a moment longer, still coming down from her orgasm, but the ice melted away from his fingers as if it had never been there, wetness now coating them. They were so damn cold. He tucked his hand under his arm and clenched his teeth, trying to get his fingers warm.

Even if he lost them due to frostbite, it'd be worth every moment. The look on her face as she come had been stunning.

Feeling slowly returned to his fingers, followed by an awful aching tingle, and then hot slivers of pain creeping over his skin. He pressed his arm against his hand, trying to produce more heat, and was silent as she sat up, dazed, pushing her messy hair out of her face. The look on her lovely features was sated, pleased, and so soft that he wanted to kiss her. More than that, he wanted that sweet mouth on his cock, but the pain shooting through his unfrozen fingers warned him off of that idea.

"You didn't come, did you, Kai?" she asked softly, her legs falling back together and hiding her sweet core from him.

"I enjoyed seeing you get release," he said gruffly, trying to ignore the throb of his painful hand. It was bad. Real bad, but he'd survive it. "I'm fine."

She bit her lip, as if considering his words. Then, she crawled forward on the bed to where he was, her cool breath puffing in the icy air. Her fingers grazed down one furs-covered arm, playing with the skins. "Can I wear your mitten?"

He tilted his head, watching her, curious.

Her eyes shone with excitement and arousal as she looked up at him. "I want to pleasure you like you did me."

Kai's breath caught in his throat. She was a powerful sorceress and he was nothing but her captive...and yet that was it and wasn't it anymore. But to have this beautiful, sensual woman who held so much power want to put on his glove and give him pleasure like he'd given her? He was still surprised.

Surprised, and aching with need.

She took his mitten before he could say anything, and he was fascinated by the delicate movements of her fingers as she tugged it on. Then, she flexed her hand and gave him an impish look. "Can I touch you now?"

Wordless, he nodded.

She crawled over toward him on the bed and considered his clothing. He was still wrapped, head to toe, in his makeshift fur garments. Charlotte considered them, and then tilted her head at him. "Do you want to undress for me?"

He did. Gods have mercy, did he ever.

Kai tugged at the leather straps holding the fur tunic against his body. He undid the knots with shaking fingers even as she reached between his thighs and cupped the bulge of his erection, as if impatient for him to ready for her. "Oh, Kai," she breathed. "Just look at you. You feel so big."

He felt as if he was going to explode in her hand if she started stroking him, but he needed her touch so badly he didn't care. He groaned and jerked at the knots, tearing the furs from his body now. He had to get free from the confining feel of them, needed her hand on him...however much he could handle. It didn't matter that there was a furry glove separating his cock from her cool fingers. He just needed her touch.

When the furs were stripped from his body, he undid the knot that held his loincloth in place. The soft suede-cloth fell away, and his cock sprang free, erect and aching. The head was purple with need, and he could practically see blood throbbing under the skin.

"Oh wow," Charlotte said, her voice soft. Her gloved hand closed around him, the fur tickling the sensitive skin of his groin. "You're so big. God, I wish I could put my mouth on you. It's practically watering at the sight of all this." Her hand pumped gently.

He fell back into the bed with a groan. "Charlotte. Do not tease me."

"No, I won't," she said quickly. Her hand tightened around his shaft. "I want to see you come. I want to please you...like you pleased me."

Just her touch pleased him, and he wanted to tell her that, but she gave his cock another squeeze and then began to pump him again, and it was too much. He'd been waiting so long for her touch that he was ready to spill his seed at her soft grip, the ticklish touch of the fox fur. "Work me with your sweet hand," he commanded, and she immediately began to pump him faster.

It was enough. With a hiss of breath, he came, his seed erupting and splashing across the glove. She gasped and jerked away, and his own hand replaced hers, milking the last of his orgasm as he came down, blackness swimming before his eyes. He'd never come so hard, and all of this from a quick jerk from a gloved hand.

Imagine if she could truly touch him. The thought made a fresh wave of come erupt, and he finished working himself with his hand, fingers sticky with his own spend. With a heavy, final sigh, he opened his eyes and looked over at her.

She was dabbing at her bare chest with one of the furs, tears freezing into tracks on the sides of her face.

"Charlotte?"

"I'm fine," she said quickly, smoothing a hand over her skin. As quick as her touch, she iced up, her clothing forming again.

But not fast enough - he saw the red, blistered streak across her breast. Kai reached for her, shocked. "Did I do that to you?"

"It...it must have splashed. I'm fine. Really. The ice on it feels better." She gave him a faint smile and lifted her chin in his direction. "Is your hand okay?"

It throbbed like fire, actually. He extended it toward her. Mottled white, red, and yellow patches covered his skin. Charlotte gasped again. "Your hand!"

"It's fine." He hoped it was fine, at least. "It will be better in a day or two. I promise."

Her eyes swam with tears and she gave him a woebegone look. "Was it a mistake for us to touch each other?"

Ignoring the itching throb of his hand, he picked up his fur cape and gently wrapped it around her, and then hugged her close, their skin protected. "I wish my seed had not burned your soft skin. That, I would change. Otherwise, I would not change a moment of it if I could, Charlotte. Every caress was special to me."

"Me too," she admitted softly, snuggling against him as much as she could. "I just wish..."

"I know." He sighed heavily, thinking of what it would be like to truly hold her against his bare chest and touch her freely. "I know."

Chapter Seven

A week later

"Kai! Where are you? Come see!" Charlotte pushed through one of the ice walls, searching for Kai. "I did it!"

"Did what?" he asked, leaving the area they'd come to start calling the 'Ice Kitchen'. He'd caught a snow rabbit in a snare earlier that day and was preparing the meat for cooking, since the soups that her servants brought were filling but not particularly tasty. He'd started hunting once they'd returned from the mountains, and just outside the walls of the castle, he'd set up multiple snares. So far, each day, he'd yielded results, which pleased both of them.

If there was still game in the area, after all, maybe eternal snow wouldn't be such a problem.

"Come see," she said excitedly, reaching for him.

He grimaced at his bloody hands, dunked them in a nearby bucket of water that she'd unfrozen for him earlier, and then tugged on a glove. When he was armored against her touch, Kai put his hand in hers and let her lead him through the castle. She headed straight forward, ignoring rooms and corridors and just melting walls as she saw fit. Kai followed close at her side, and the ice walls reformed as they passed through.

"You need to use doors," Kai teased. "Save your magic. You're expending too much strength."

She was, it was true. But she'd been so excited about her latest project that she hadn't thought, she'd simply raced to find him. Dutifully, Charlotte headed down the long corridor to the front gate, eschewing her wall-melting and had the massive icy doors open to admit her outside. "Now come and see what I've done," she said excitedly, pulling him to one side of the courtyard.

Row after row of frozen earth had been uncovered. They'd worked together over two days to make the tiny, naked garden that Charlotte now viewed proudly. De-icing it had been an easy job for Charlotte. They'd made an ice plow and had taken turns dragging it across the frozen ground to make rows. It had been difficult work, but Kai's company had made it pleasant work.

And from there, Charlotte had begun her week-long struggle. Her magic was in ice and water, but she was pressing herself outward, extending the boundaries of what she could and couldn't do. If snow and ice were her domain, maybe she could learn to master things that lived in this realm, too. So she'd set to work. For a day or two, she'd explored the nearby areas looking for plants that were still alive despite the snowy weather. She'd found one wizened fruit bush with tiny, unripe berries on it. That had been enough - she'd taken cuttings back, as well as the berries, and had set to work in the garden.

Every minute, every hour of the day, she sank her magic into those small plants. She didn't know how to manipulate the plants, but if it was anything like her ice magic, all she had to do was concentrate and will it to be so. So she sat at the edge of the field, and stared.

And stared. And focused her magic on those berries and stems in the ground. She packed them with snow and melted it so the ground was wet, and infused even more magic into the soil. She pumped so much magic into those stupid patches of dirt that she went to bed every night, utterly exhausted, her head throbbing. Every ounce of her energy was spent in trying to make those plants grow. Meanwhile, her castle fortifications were forgotten in lieu of more important projects, like how to feed a starving people.

On day one, she planted the berries and was filled with determination and hope.

On days two and three, she worked hard.

By day four, she was ready to collapse. The ground showed no signs of life, and the seeds weren't responding.

On day five, tiny sprouts started to show amidst the snow. She gave them a little push with her magic and was gleeful when they'd responded by surging in height. Given enough magic, she could make these plants respond to her will just like the water and ice would.

Her plan was working. Exuberant, she'd retrieved Kai and showed him the fruits of her labors. "It's working!"

He stared down at the small greens barely poking through the ground. "Are those..."

"Berry bushes! Yes! Give me enough time and I bet I can make them grow strong and produce fruit. And if we can do this with one plant, we can do this with others." Her hands clutched his gloved one excitedly. "No one has to starve or go without. We can make this place as fertile with snow as it is without."

Kai looked down at her and grinned. Then, he whooped with joy and threw his arms around her, grabbing her and spinning her around in a tinkle of icy skirts.

Charlotte giggled, ecstatic with joy. All the hard work of the last week, all the awful headaches were forgotten in that moment. Right now, there was only hope.

"You're incredible, Charlotte," he said, putting her down again.

She smiled at him and her knees wobbled as her feet touched the ground, and she sank against his legs. God, she was weak.

He caught her with his hands and went down with her. "Charlotte! Are you all right?"

"Just tired," she said with a faint smile.

"You've been pushing too hard," he chided, helping her back to her feet. "It won't do anyone any good if you destroy yourself trying to fix things."

Actually, that would probably solve the problem of having a snow queen in residence, Charlotte thought, but kept that to herself. He was right, she was pushing too hard. She was just so desperate to see any kind of result that she'd been pouring heart and soul into things.

"Let me carry you," he said, picking her up again and hauling her into his arms. "Come inside and eat. You need your strength."

"I'll be fine," she protested. "I just need a moment to rest and then I can go back to work."

"No more work for now," he said firmly. "Rest."

"We don't have time to rest." Her fingers curled into the soft furs he wore and for a heart-wrenching moment, she wished it was his skin she was touching. Just once. "They're going to be coming for me and I need to show them that I'm not totally evil."

He shook his head. "Even if you believe this, I'm not sure I do. Regardless, you won't be able to do anything if you don't take care of yourself." He carried her through the icy halls, pausing at each door and opening it. It felt painfully slow to Charlotte, who was used to just melting them along the way, but she suddenly felt weak, exhausted, and tapped out. Maybe he was right.

101

When they got to Charlotte's bedroom, Kai gently laid her down in bed. "Just rest," he told her softly. She felt him press his scorching mouth to her hair and felt the strands lifting as he pulled away. She looked up, startled, and her hair was stuck to his mouth, frozen. For some reason, that struck her as wildly funny and she began to giggle as he cursed under his breath.

"I hate that I cannot touch you," he swore, furious. "Not even to comfort you."

Suddenly it wasn't funny any longer. Charlotte's laughter died as quickly as it had arrived. For the last week, they'd been in a hellish touch-but-don't-touch sort of scenario. From their heavy petting session, Kai's hand had blistered and swollen and taken days to recover. Her own sensitive skin had taken almost as long to heal. Those welts had been a reminder to be careful, and they'd been more cautious in their affection toward one another. They hadn't gone as far as before - not daring to - but the constant need lingered between them like an unfulfilled ache. Instead, they caressed and petted and touched...all within the safe confines of covered skin.

It was driving Charlotte crazy. And if it drove her crazy, it had to be driving Kai wild as well.

But they were stuck. There was nothing they could do about it.

Sometimes, Charlotte secretly hoped that if she expended enough magic, she'd warm up a few degrees. Just enough for Kai's skin to touch her own. But no matter how tirelessly she worked, she never seemed to exhaust her magic. Sometimes it sputtered weakly because she'd tapped herself out, but there was always a reserve. And she never, ever warmed up a degree.

So what could she do? She had an ice palace in the middle of a country that didn't want her there. She had a man she was attracted to and who was also attracted to her...who she couldn't touch. And in a few days, there would be a murdering mob on her doorstep ready to take said man away from her and possibly end her life...unless she ended theirs first.

All in all, it was a pretty shitty situation. So what could she do? She worked on her plants, she cuddled with Kai, and she did her best not to think about the future.

Two days before the end of the month, Charlotte was out working in the garden when Muffin returned.

A vision in a puffy pink parka, snow skis, and what looked like yellow cowboy boots, the fairy godmother dug her poles into the earth and skied directly over Charlotte's poor plants.

Charlotte gave a shriek of horror and tried to coax one berry plant out from under Muffin's crushing neon pink ski. "What are you doing?"

"I might ask the same of you, young lady!" The fairy godmother sounded irate. "I thought we talked about this? You're the snow queen. Not Martha Stewart! Now, what's with the gardening?"

"Get off my plants and I'll tell you."

Muffin did, but not before bonking Charlotte on the head with one of her ski poles. "I am not impressed, Charlotte. Not impressed at all."

Charlotte ignored Muffin's bad mood and sank her fingers back into the icy soil, pushing magic around the wounded plants to bolster them again. The greens were growing, but were spindly and pale, and needed constant attention. She'd been working so hard on them this last week and they were showing signs of berries. If she just kept pushing them and coaxing them a bit more, they'd get there...

"Charlotte, I am concerned about you." Muffin tapped on her head with the ski pole again, but gently. "I worry you're not going to be ready in two days. You do know what happens in two days, don't you?"

She packed dirt around one listing little plant and gave it an extra push with her magic, and was pleased when it perked up. "Gerda comes here looking for me."

"Looking for your head on a pike," Muffin corrected, and lifted one of the ends of her ski-poles and pointed it toward Charlotte's throat. "And you don't seem concerned."

"Oh, I'm concerned," Charlotte said. "That's why I'm working so hard on these." She gestured at the tidy rows of pale little plants. One or two of the heartier ones were even starting to resemble bushes. She was getting there. She just needed more time.

"Where's your captive boy-toy?"

"He's out ice fishing. And he's not my captive," Charlotte said. "Not any longer. He stays because he wants to, now."

"Oh, that's adorable," Muffin said sarcastically. "Is it true love?" When Charlotte's cheeks colored, Muffin groaned. "Oh honey, no. I told you to use him for sex. Strap on a big ice dildo and have him call you 'sir'. Have a good time with him! Tickle his undercarriage! Tweak his manly little nipples! But no hearts allowed."

Okay, that was embarrassing. Charlotte pressed the backs of her hands to her hot cheeks. "You have a salty mouth for a fairy godmother."

"And you have weird ideas for a snow queen," Muffin returned. She nodded at the icy courtyard. "Come. Take a walk with me."

This was going to be a lecture, Charlotte suspected. Still, Muffin controlled everything here and Charlotte had to obey. She stood, brushed off her hands on her crystalline skirts, and then trotted behind Muffin as she started to ski away.

The fairy godmother skied to one of the outer walls and then began to slow. Her skis changed to snowshoes with a flutter of glitter, and then Muffin began to tromp along the snowy edge. She still had her ski poles, so Charlotte moved alongside her, just out of reach of another thwap with a pole in case her mood was still sour.

"You've been here almost a month now, correct?"

"That's right," Charlotte said.

"And you knew about Gerda coming the entire time. I filled you in on how the fairy tale goes."

She didn't know where Muffin was heading with this. "Right..."

Muffin turned to Charlotte, and her wrinkled, round little face was unhappy. "I give you a hard time, Charlotte dear, but I like you. That's why I don't want to see you fail."

A cold clench moved around Charlotte's heart. "Well," she said, trying to keep her voice light. "I don't really want to fail either."

Muffin shook her head, took another step forward, and then prodded one of the ice walls of the courtyard with her ski-pole. "What does this look like to you?"

Was this a trick question? "Um...ice? An ice wall?"

"And what is the purpose of a wall?"

"To keep things out?"

Muffin's ski pole prodded the wall again, this time a bit harder. A chunk of ice fell to the ground and left a fist-sized hole in Charlotte's wall, where she could see out the other side. "Here's the thing with ice, sweetie. On sunny days, it melts." Muffin gestured at the clear blue sky overhead. "You want your ice fortress to remain a fortress? You need to stay on top of things. I thought you were fortifying the castle?"

"I am! I was. I just, um, got distracted."

"By plants? Or by the boy toy?"

"Both?" Charlotte grimaced. "But there's a reason behind the plants, I swear. I—"

Muffin jabbed at the ice wall again and an even larger chunk fell down at Charlotte's feet. Okay, now she was starting to get annoyed with the fairy godmother. Did she have to do that right now? "Your ice fortress is one good push away from falling apart," Muffin told her. "And what are you going to do then?"

Charlotte opened her mouth to protest, but another chunk fell from the wall several feet away. It landed with a wet splat. No one had touched it. Frowning, she stepped toward the wall and put her hand on it to patch up...and felt just how weak it was. The ice molecules (or whatever she was feeling when she touched it) seemed sluggish and thin. She gave it a push of her own magic...and was alarmed at the faint sputter of her own response. She'd been pouring too much of herself into the plants and she had nothing left to repair her home. "I...I'll fix it later, When I've rested."

"Charlotte, honey, this is such a bad idea! Can't you see that? I'm worried about you. Just because you accidentally landed as the bad guy doesn't mean that I want you to fail."

Why was Muffin so sure that Charlotte was going to fail? It was making her uneasy. "But things are different this time. I'm going to talk to Gerda. Show her the plants I'm growing. It'll make a difference, I know it will. We can all come to peaceful terms over this—"

Muffin shook her head solemnly.

"—what?"

"Honey." Muffin's little hand patted at Charlotte's icy sleeve, and then stuck there. The fairy godmother frowned, blew a cloud of glitter at her hand, and unstuck it. She shook her fingers in the air, as if restoring circulation. "I keep forgetting about that."

"I didn't," Charlotte said in a wry, sad voice. It made her feel more despair every time someone reached to touch her.

"Honey," Muffin said again. "This is not my first go-around in this fairy tale. I've had my share of Snow Queen stories. And while I admit this is the first time I've been working from the other side, there is one consistent factor in things."

Charlotte's stomach gave an uneasy little flip. "What's that?"

"No one ever loses against the snow queen. Gerda always wins. Always. *Always.*" She gave her head a little shake, the puffy pink parka rustling. "Why do you think we have the interns start with this sort of fairy tale? Because it's a 'gimme' for them. It's training wheels. You set your girl as Gerda, and Gerda always, always defeats the snow queen. Later on, we move them to something more challenging." Muffin wrinkled her nose, thinking. "Might be a while before Fifi moves on to something challenging, I have to admit."

She swallowed hard, that sick feeling in her stomach growing. "But if I'm the first snow queen, maybe I can be the first winner."

The look Muffin gave her shut that concept down. "By, what? Tossing those weak little plants at her?"

"I want to show her that I'm here to do good—"

"And you think she'll stop in her avenging rampage long enough to listen? As you continue to hold Kai captive at your side?"

"He's not my captive!"

"He's still here, isn't he? He's not home, helping them with the hunt or feeding hungry families? Because you know there are hungry families. His people aren't used to the cold. Look at the tan on that boy. That's not the mark of someone who spends his days tromping through the snow."

Charlotte swallowed. Bent her head in defeat. "I...just wanted things to be different. I didn't want to be the bad guy."

"I know sweetie." Muffin gave her another little pat, this time with a gloved hand. "You mean well, and I get that you're trying to make the best of a bad situation. I get that. I really do. But you're better off preparing the fortress for the invaders instead of trying to grow flowers. I'm just trying to help because I hate to see you go down without a fight. And the way you are headed? You are in for a quick and humiliating defeat."

Charlotte nodded, head bent. Tears pricked at her eyes but she struggled to keep them back. She didn't want to cry in front of the fairy godmother.

"As for that boy toy of yours. It's clear to see that you've become attached. I know you've been lonely, darling, but you need to cut the cord before someone gets hurt."

Too late, Charlotte thought. But she forced herself to swallow the knot in her throat. "Cut the cord?"

"Yes. Let's extrapolate our future scenarios for a minute, shall we?" Muffin's mittened hand soothed Charlotte's bent back. "Let's say Gerda shows up two days from now, as we know she's going to. There are two possible outcomes. The most likely one is that you lose, right? And what do you think is going to happen to that boy when he sees his childhood friend cut your head off and raise it on a pike at the castle gates?"

Charlotte gasped and put a hand to her throat. "She's going to what?"

Muffin blinked, looking alarmed. "Hyperbole! We don't know that's going to happen. Maybe she'll just burn you at the stake like a witch or something more dignified. It varies depending on the flavor of Gerda."

"Great," Charlotte enthused tonelessly.

"Either way, how do you think that boy's going to feel?"

Charlotte said nothing. She didn't want to think about how Kai was going to feel at the sight of her dead. If he really, truly cared for her...he'd be devastated. As devastated as she would be if he got hurt in the upcoming inevitable battle. "He'll be safe either way, won't he?"

"Well," Muffin hedged.

She turned an alarmed look at the fairy godmother. "Won't he?"

"I'm not going to lie to you; sometimes things go badly in the final battle. I've seen some incarnations of Kai trapped in the ice palace when the Queen goes down and he's buried alive. I've seen him accidentally stabbed by his own people's spears in the heat of the battle. I've seen the queen kill him out of spite. But a lot of the time he lives." Muffin gave her a bright smile. "Mostly. It just depends on how this story plays out."

But she was always doomed. And her doom might affect Kai. In addition to hurting his heart, she might cost him his life. She needed to fix that. "I see."

"I think you're starting to," Muffin said. "Now, let's extrapolate some more, shall we? Let's say that we roll the dice and you fight Gerda and you hit that one in a million chance and win this thing. Wouldn't that be nice?" Muffin beamed at her, but Charlotte couldn't even muster a return smile. "Then, we whisk you out of here, lickety split, and set you in your nice, new, cozy reality where you'll spend the rest of your life."

Wait...what? "New reality?"

"Well, yes. You didn't think you were going to stay here, did you? Once the fairy tale is over?"

Actually, she *had* thought that. Charlotte sniffed. "W-what happens if I win, then?"

109

"You get a new, fresh start in an entirely new place. Just nice, normal you in a nice, normal place. No fairy tale, just the happy ever after part. Think of it as Charlotte 2.0."

She blinked repeatedly, unable to process this. No more snow queen? No more endless winter and ice and powers? No polar bears for mounts. No unseen servants to serve her and no icy boudoir to sleep in. No ice gowns. She'd be normal. She'd be able to be touched and be loved, and to touch and love back.

But...Kai. "I...what if I want to stay here?"

"Not possible." Muffin pinched her cheek with a mittened thumb. "You don't really think these people are going to want a snow queen around forever, do you?"

"I'd kind of hoped..."

"Don't be silly."

She licked her dry lips. "What...if I win, does the old snow queen take her body back over again?"

"That's need-to-know information, Charlotte darling, and you really do not need to know."

That didn't sound good. Oh, Kai, Kai. Would he even know it wasn't her before it was too late? Or would he end up trapped all over again?

Oh dear lord, what could she do to fix this? Charlotte looked around at her crumbling, melting walls. At the patchy ice that had - two weeks ago - been the start of a rather fierce and forbidding ice fortress. At the limp plants in neat rows that she'd spent so much time and energy on.

Boy, she'd really fucked this one up, hadn't she?

Charlotte stared blankly at the walls. "I've got a lot of work to do in the next two days."

Muffin beamed at her. "I can see my little pep talk helped. You scrape yourself off the ground, Charlotte dearie, and you get back to work. There's always hope, right? And you'll want to go down swinging."

"I'll get started," she said, an ache in her throat that wouldn't go away. "You can count on me."

"Good job," Muffin said, and waved one of her ski poles in the air. "I'm out of here, then. See you in a few days!" She vanished in a puff of glitter.

Charlotte sank to her knees, a small moan escaping her throat.

What could she do? She had two days and her ice castle was crumbling around her. Her ice magic was ebbing low, because she'd sunk so much of it into her plants. Those stupid, stupid plants. If she wanted a shot in hell of sticking around to become Charlotte 2.0, she needed to redo her ice walls. Make them stronger, thicker. Maybe create some icy pit traps around the courtyard with some ice spikes at the bottom...

She shuddered, mentally picturing someone that looked like Kai stumbling into an icy pit trap. Could she do that? Could she embrace her evil side in order to survive? She had to - if she didn't, she'd be annihilated right out of the afterlife. The cards were stacked against her no matter what she did.

And oh God. What if she hurt Kai in the process? She looked back at her ice castle, not seeing it as a glimmering, secure fortress but an icy creation one strong gust of wind away from collapsing. What if one of the icy crenellations collapsed under the heat of the sun and pinned him underneath? What if the entire thing came crashing down when she bit it?

Worse, what if the old queen returned and Kai went to her with open arms, thinking it was Charlotte?

She had to do something. Something different. She had to fix this. God, she'd made such a mess of things, even worse than that stupid Fifi. Desperate, she clutched at the frosty mounds of her skirts and pushed her way inside the front doors of the castle, seeing now just how fragile and ephemeral her dwelling was. It was no place to keep Kai safe. The ice could collapse on top of her and not hurt her, but Kai was all too warm and human and fragile for this. She thought of his warm brown skin, smothered in furs so he didn't freeze to death.

She thought of his blistered hand, frost nipped from where he'd touched her. He'd nearly lost his fingers, all because he'd wanted to pleasure her.

A sob escaped Charlotte's throat. She was selfishly destroying him and his life, wasn't she? Even without the mirror chips in his eyes, she was still manipulating him.

The mirror.

Gasping, Charlotte ran for the deepest recesses of the snow queen's secret chambers. She found the thick wall behind her throne, coaxed it open, and then staggered through. There, set alone, was the magic mirror. It oozed power and malevolence. The two chips that had been in Kai's eyes were returned, and the glass itself was unblemished perfection.

A fine mist seemed to cling to the air around the mirror. She approached it cautiously. It felt dirty to stand so close to it, like she was breathing in oily, unctuous evil with every breath.

But there was power here. Lots and lots of power. And Charlotte's power was running low. The mirror might be able to save her.

Licking her lips nervously, she took another step forward and stared into the mirror's reflection. There was her face, so pale and frightened, surrounded by a wild tangle of pale blonde hair. Her skin had a bluish, frosty tinge to it, but the mirror made it seem sickly, unholy. Everything about the mirror made her skin crawl. Her mind rebelled at the thought of touching it, using it, but she was running out of options fast.

"Hello?" Charlotte said softly. "Are you there?"

Alwaysss...

Yeah, that wasn't encouraging. "Um. I think I need your help."

I am here...speak what you need...

She looked down at her hands. They were trembling, but she wasn't sure if it was anxiety or fear or just exhaustion. "I need more magic. I need to fortify the walls here because I need to protect myself."

Tell me what you will give me...

Charlotte frowned. "Give you?"

All magic requires a trade...

That sounded horribly ominous. "And if I have nothing to give you?"

Don't you?

An uncomfortable prickle touched her skin. She took a step away from the mirror. "What do you mean? I don't have anything except ice and magic, and I'm coming to you for more of those."

Twin pricks of light centered in the mirror, right over the spot where her eyes were. You removed these once. You can replace them again.

"In Kai?" she asked, horrified. "They made him a zombie!"

He is strong. You can use him to feed your own magic.

"No! There has to be another way!"

This time, the mirror's tone was mocking and evil. Where do you think magic comes from, little one? Power must come from somewhere, even borrowed power. You've used me once before...

"Not me! Never me!"

Ah, but you are not so different from the other queen. She came to me seeking power as well...

And she'd done whatever it took to get that power. Charlotte squeezed her eyes shut, but when she did, all she saw was Kai's mirrored, deadened gaze. "I can't do that to him."

113

Can't you? He trusts you. All you need is to get close enough to touch him and I'll do the rest. He won't even notice...

Because his mind would be turned to mush. Charlotte shuddered. She wanted to leave - run away - but the power pulsing in the mirror was real and thick in the air and she was running out of options. "Tell me something else I can do. Anything. Just...not that."

You make it sound as if you have choices...

That made her angry. "I always have choices, you son of a bitch. I can choose what I want to do. I'm in charge of this fairy tale at the moment."

The mirror said nothing, but she could hear the echo of its laughter in her mind.

"Forget it," she said, turning away. "I'll figure out something else."

You'll be back. The other always was...

For some reason, that sent a chill down her spine. God, what if the snow queen had started out as another, normal woman and had turned to the mirror for help? What if it had corrupted her? What if that happened to Charlotte?

What if, in two days, she grew weak with fear?

No, she told herself, shaking her head. She would never do that to Kai. But if someone else came close...

Oh God. What was she thinking? She wouldn't sacrifice someone else just to drag a few more days out of her own sorry life. The very thought horrified her. She turned and looked at the mirror. Just being in its presence made her want a bath. She felt dirty from being near it. Dirty from having talked to it. Like its evil was worming its way through her system.

Twin gleams remained in the mirror's glass, reminding her of what it wanted.

There was only one way to fix this. Charlotte dredged up enough power to make an ice club. She approached the mirror slowly, hefting it.

You won't do it, the mirror mocked. Where do you think you get this limitless power from already? Your predecessor has sacrificed many a slave to increase her pool—

The mirror made a delightful shattering sound when the club hit it. Shards rained down on the floor, and for a moment, Charlotte could almost see the evil miasma hang in the air like a puff of smoke. Then, it dissipated and the room brightened.

The ominous, heavy pulse of magic in the room was gone.

And so was Charlotte's strength. As if someone had pulled the plug on her power, all of the energy left her body. She collapsed on the floor, too weak to hold up the club.

How...why was she suddenly so weak? Had she - the old snow queen - really borrowed that much power from the mirror? And here Charlotte had been expending it right and left, as if it were limitless. Right now, she didn't even feel as if she had enough energy to get up and walk across the floor, much less reinforce the falling walls around the castle.

Things were quickly going from bad to worse. Angry tears threatened, but Charlotte sniffed them away. All right. She didn't have much power left. She had two days before Gerda would come here, and she could prepare. She could do lots of things...

Hell, who was she kidding? She was screwed and a half. She flopped onto her back and stared up at the ceiling of her ice palace. The carefully crafted prisms gleamed with cold, incredibly beautiful and ethereal.

A drop of meltwater fell from the ceiling and plopped on her cheek.

Figured. If the roof was going to cave in in the next day or two, it'd serve her right. Just because she didn't want to be the bad guy in the fairy tale. Well, she'd destroyed her magic mirror, and she was still the bad guy, and she was going to lose, lose, lose.

These two days might be her last days here, waiting while the palace collapsed slowly around her. She...

She paused. Sat up.

She had to get Kai out of here.

Chapter Eight

Kai was whistling when he returned to the ice fortress, a string of fat fish over his shoulder. Her suggestion to cut a hole into the ice and fish there had worked splendidly, and he'd caught them a magnificent, fresh dinner. Granted, Charlotte's would have to ice hers down to enjoy it, but it would be a treat for both of them after weeks of colored cubes and the nutrient broth of his. He couldn't wait to see the expression on her face when he showed her his catch. Then, he'd bake them over an open fire and make her eat until she could eat no more. She'd been pushing herself hard these last few days and she looked exhausted.

He knelt and slipped back through the hole she'd crafted for him through the wall. So much for his being her captive, he thought with a wry smile. When had that stopped being a thing between them? Ever since she walked down to the cave and pulled the mirrors from his eyes, she'd been different. Sweet. Funny. Caring. Now, he didn't stay with her because he'd been ensorcelled - he stayed because he cared for her.

She was convinced that in two days, Gerda would come traipsing up the mountain looking for him and looking to make an end of her. He wasn't so sure about that. Sure, Gerda was an impulsive girl, but to confront someone with the magnitude of Charlotte's powers would be foolishness itself. Even Gerda wasn't that naive.

To his surprise, she wasn't in the courtyard when he entered. He called out her name, "Charlotte?" Sometimes she was just an ice-wall away and would melt through the moment she 'felt' him enter. But today, there was no welcoming greeting. A prickle of unease touched him, and he dropped his fish onto a snowbank, heading into the castle.

When he touched the massive entryway door, it felt slick under his glove. Was it melting? He squinted up at the skies, which were sunny but as cold as ever. Huh. With a heave, Kai pushed the thick ice open and stepped into the palace. "Charlotte?"

No answer. His footsteps increased in pace and he began to race through the halls. Had she somehow hurt herself? Used so much of her powers that she'd knocked herself unconscious? Finally wore herself out? He headed for the bedroom, where they slept curled together every night, never quite touching.

She was there, tucked into the bed they shared, a tiny figure in a nest of ice and furs.

"Charlotte?" he called again.

She sat up, brushing at her face. It was obvious he'd woken her from a slumber. It was also obvious there was something wrong. She looked weak, pale. Normally there was an almost unhealthy radiance to her, as if she were lit from within with magic. That light had been snuffed. The girl in front of him seemed incredibly fragile.

"What's wrong? You look..." he paused, unsure what to say. Different? Sick? Pale? "Unwell." Unease swept through him. What if...what if she'd changed again?

118

What if this was no longer Charlotte but the other queen again?

Or worse...what if it was someone else entirely? He studied her warily.

The smile she gave him was wan. "I'm fine," she told him. "But we need to talk."

He didn't like the way she slowly got out of bed, as if every muscle ached. He didn't like the reluctant way she shrugged on one of the furs over her body. Normally she bounded out of bed, full of energy, reshaping her ice-gown into something beautiful and artistic full of crystalline facets. The gown she wore now was cracked from where she'd lain on it and as he watched, a piece of the skirt shattered and fell away, revealing one pale foot. "You need to rest. You've been working yourself too hard."

She shook her head. "I'm fine. Really. But, Kai—"

"Charlotte," he said firmly. "You—"

"I'm releasing you."

He paused. "You're what?"

"I'm releasing you," she said, her voice weary. "You need to go. Leave the castle today."

"What about you?"

"I'm staying here until...until the end."

That sounded so incredibly fatalistic that he grew concerned. "Charlotte, you're sick. I'm not leaving your side—"

This time, she shook her head violently. "You're not listening to me. You have to leave. Now. I'm releasing you! Go back to your people. You don't have to stay with me."

"Of course I don't have to stay with you." What in all the names of the gods was she babbling about? "I'm here because I'm—" he paused, not sure what to call their relationship. In his culture, a man didn't touch a woman like he'd touched Charlotte unless they were wedded.

He'd assumed that since they were together emotionally if not physically, she was his mate in all but the ceremony. But she'd not approached the concept of mating. He knew she wasn't from a people like his own...did they even have mates? Did they wed or did they simply go about their lives by themselves? Because he sure as damn well thought of her as his mate.

And now she was sending him away? The thought was inconceivable.

So he said, "I'm not going anywhere."

Charlotte frowned up at him. "Kai, don't argue with me. Not about this."

"We won't argue, then." He began to thrust his hand into one of his mittens so he could touch her and help her stand up. "I'm not going anywhere."

"You are. I don't want you here," she protested.

"Lies." He bit at the laces on his mitts, tightening them, "I'm going to make you dinner and I'm going to feed you, and then we'll talk about this—"

"No," she said again, and drew herself to her feet. Her eyes gleamed with a shimmer of ice - were those tears? - and then she clenched her fists at her sides. "This is for your own good, Kai. Leave this place and return to your people or I'm going to make you leave. You don't belong here."

"Leave?" He snorted. "You are my mate. I'm not going anywhere."

"I can't be your mate," she gritted. He felt her drawing magic, drawing power closer to her. Her brow broke out in a shiny glimmer of crystalized sweat beads. "We can't even touch."

"That doesn't matter. I can touch you," he snarled. "Shall I show you how much I can touch you? Shall I make you come again? Make you cry out my name as I pump my fingers into you?"

"And then you lose your hand because it freezes off? I won't let you do that." She raised her hands in the air. "And if you won't leave, I'll make you leave."

The ice surged around his feet, trapping them.

"Charlotte, no," he growled. "Don't do this."

"I'm sorry," she said. "But I have to." And the ice surged around him, carrying him like a wave. New bursts of ice formed on her forehead, and she swayed as she reshaped the walls and pushed him, protesting, right out of the castle itself and into the courtyard. From there, the tidal wave of ice continued, pushing him, pushing him, pushing him right out of her domain. With a hoarse cry, he tumbled to the earth as it dumped him outside of the protective wall surrounding the courtyard. As he got to his feet, the ice surged back into place, resealing the wall and trapping him outside.

He slammed a fist into the ice. "Charlotte," he yelled. "Don't do this!"

There was no response. She'd shut him out entirely.

For hours, Kai pounded at the wall, determined to make Charlotte notice him. When dusk fell, he gathered firewood, rubbed sticks until he made a fire, and camped out at her doorstep, waiting for her to return. To apologize and let him in. To flounce out in a swirl of icy skirts and yell at him so they could at least talk.

Something.

Anything.

But when a bitterly cold dawn crested on the horizon and Kai's fire burned through the last of the wood he'd gathered, and the ice keep was utterly silent, he realized that she wouldn't be relenting after all. With a heavy heart, he gathered his furs tight against his body, snuffed his fire, and began to walk to his people's village.

It took him most of a day to follow the cook fires to where they'd created their lodges anew. Charlotte's castle was in the heart of the territory that they claimed for their tribe, but they'd moved away from the edges of the sea and its bounty to the edges of the valley, where food was scarce and snow was thick on the ground.

Someone hailed him as he approached, and Kai raised a weary hand in greeting. Moments later, others in the tribe approached, swarming him with hugs and happy greetings. They were excited to see him return, hale and healthy, and he wished he could share the excitement in their voices. Instead, he kept thinking of Charlotte, the way she'd pushed him out. Her fragility as she'd sat up on the bed when he'd last seen her.

Something in her had changed, and not for the better, and he was worried she'd somehow used too much magic and hurt herself. And even though Kajeh hugged him close, chief Dovak whacked him on the back with relief, and little Tidda patted him with tiny hands to reassure herself that he was back, he didn't feel like he was at home.

At some point, home had become the high, crystalline walls of the palace and Charlotte's sweet smile.

And even as he mused on this, a woman approached, her own body wrapped in thick tailored leathers, her long black braids dancing on her shoulders. Gerda smiled at him and hugged him close, and her lovely face was radiant. "Kai! You are back!"

"For now," he agreed.

She frowned at that tepid response. Linking her arm in his, she tugged him toward the fire burning outside of her small hut. "How did you escape? Will the evil bitch come looking for you?"

"She's not evil—" he began.

Gerda immediately grabbed his face and began to study his eyes.

He swatted her hand away. "The mirrors are gone. They haven't been there for a while. That wasn't her that did that."

Gerda's eyes widened. "There is more than one snow bitch?"

"No, there's just the one," he corrected, irritated at her words. "And she's not a bitch. She's kind. I think she's...ensorcelled herself." Kai thought of the mysterious people she'd begged and pleaded with in the middle of the night, who disappeared when he hunted for them. "Someone has trapped her, like I was trapped. And she let me go."

"I don't understand."

No, she wouldn't. And he wasn't explaining it right. How could he possibly tell Gerda that while the snow queen looked the same from her cloud-pale hair to the blue tinge of her delicate cheekbones, she was completely different underneath? That one day he'd woken up and she'd changed, so completely and utterly that even he couldn't explain it? He shook his head. "It is a long tale, for another time, and one I don't wish to share right now."

Gerda's eyes narrowed and she reached for his chin again, determined to look in his eyes.

He swatted her hand away. "Don't be childish. I'm myself."

"I don't understand you. She kidnapped you and made you her puppet. Why would she let you go? Is this a trap?"

"It's not a trap," he growled at Gerda. Normally he loved her like a sister, but tonight, he just wanted her to stop pricking at him with her sharp tongue. "Leave me be, Gerda. I've walked all day and wish nothing more than a bite of food and a bed."

But that wasn't enough for inquisitive, impulsive Gerda. "Kai?" Her voice grew soft and this time, her hand cupped his jaw. "I am truly glad to see you again. I am. But you look so very sad to be here. Aren't you happy to return?"

He closed his eyes. He wished that he was happy to be here, amongst his people again. Instead, all he could see was Charlotte's wan face, leached of all color and health, as she dragged up the last of her strength to send him away...

"I've come to care for her," he admitted to Gerda. "I've taken her as my mate, but she's pushed me away. She's sick, and I don't know how to help her because she won't let me get near her."

"I see," Gerda said softly.

He knew his words had to hurt her. Ever since they were children, it had always been assumed that Gerda and he would marry at some point, being the closest in age in their small tribe. But he'd never felt anything for Gerda except the affection one might have for a sister.

Nothing like the bleak, hopeless love he felt for Charlotte.

"Sit," Gerda said, gently steering him toward her fire and the log that served as a seat. "I've made some rabbit stew. Warm your hands and eat, and then rest. You're home."

He wasn't. But he did as she said.

The next morning, Kai awoke in a strange bed, in a strange hut, and found himself entirely too warm. He pushed the fur coverlets off him, and examined his surroundings. Gerda's hut, if the snowshoes and spears in the corner were any indication. He got to his feet, and wondered at the low murmur of voices near the central fire.

When he emerged from Gerda's hut, though, the sound of many voices grew horribly, terribly clear. The men and women of the tribe, the hunters, all carried spears and their bark shields. Great Uglaf had his prized axe resting on one shoulder. Faces were grim but determined. All had streaked their cheeks with the black paint that signified that they were going to war.

"What is this?" Kai asked, a sense of dread in his stomach.

"Return to bed, Kai," Gerda commanded. "You're not well. We will handle this."

"Handle what?" he pushed forward, ignoring Gerda's clinging hands. "Where do you go?"

"She's sick," Great Uglaf said, stroking his long braids. "You said so yourself. Now is our time to destroy her and reclaim our lands."

Destroy her? "No," Kai shouted. "She means no harm—"

The murmur of voices grew angrier. Nearby, someone shook their head with pity.

"You're still caught in her spell, Kai," Gerda said in a gentle voice. Her hands patted at his chest, as if trying to soothe him. "Let us take care of this. You will be yourself again by evening."

"I'm not sick," Kai growled, pushing her hands away. "Nor am I ensorcelled. She doesn't want to be a burden any more than we want her to. The ice covering the land isn't something she wants, either."

"Then she should leave!" said someone.

"She can't. She's trapped here," Kai said. "She must stay here until..."

Until today.

With sick horror, he stared at the war party. She was right all along. Gerda was coming for her, and only one of them would survive this day if her prophecy was correct.

And Charlotte was sick, barely able to rise from bed.

He stared at the faces of his tribe, all of them looking at him with suspicion. There was no dissuading them from their task. They were one step away from trapping him themselves, he knew, and forcing him to stay behind. He'd never let that happen. Never.

So he picked up an extra spear and clenched it in tight, bloodless fingers. "I will go with you."

Gerda's face broke into a beaming smile. "Let us go reclaim our land!" she cried, thrusting her spear into the air.

The tribe cheered. He forced himself to cheer with them.

Hopefully, somehow, Kai could protect Charlotte before it was too late.

They marched across the valley, singing battle songs and in good spirits. All of them were so positive of the outcome. Today, they would defeat the evil snow queen and reclaim their lands. Today, all would become right again.

It was all Kai could do not to howl with rage at their arrogance.

He knew they meant well. He knew this was a party to retake their land inasmuch as it was revenge for his capture. But they didn't listen when he'd tried to explain Charlotte's sweetness, her attempts to create plants to feed his people despite the cold, her loneliness and her good heart. All they saw was the snow queen.

And it was frustrating for Kai, because he couldn't blame them.

So he traveled with them in silence, ignoring the jubilant war-chants and Gerda's giddy instructions as she led the party. He needed a plan to save her before his people could harm her. She could easily protect herself by shoring up walls and turning the fortress into a maze to confuse them. She could simply shove them back out of her domain as easily as she'd removed him.

But he thought of her weakness again, and wondered how much that would cost her.

"There it is," someone murmured. Dozens of hands rose to eyes, and the war party squinted at the gleaming fortress of ice at the base of the mountain.

"It's magnificent," someone breathed. "Her power must be immense."

Kai tried to see it through their eyes, noting the delicate fluting spires that reached for the sky, the crystalline crenellations along the walls, the spikes she'd begun to create along the portcullis until she'd diverted her power otherwise.

But all Kai saw was that the castle gleamed far too wetly, too iridescent in the sunlight. The delicate, fluting spires didn't seem to be as tall as before, and the crenellations were misshapen in spots and starting to melt.

And fear pounded in his heart. Fear for Charlotte. He raced ahead, using the butt of his spear as a walking stick as he pushed through the drifting snow, heading for the castle. Gerda hurried after him, a few paces behind. "Kai?" She asked, but he ignored her. The snow underneath his feet was soft and a little slushy.

It was melting.

His heart hammered and he began to sprint. They were still several leagues from her castle, but he'd run all the gods-damned way if he had to, simply to get ahead of them. Fear carried him, made his footsteps surer than the others, made him reckless where they were cautious, and soon, he was half a league ahead of Gerda, who was shouting for him to slow down, breathless.

But on he ran.

Charlotte needed him.

It seemed like eternity before he reached the castle walls. The thick ice of the gate was locked in place, and small rivulets of meltwater ran down the front. He pushed at it, only to have his wet hands slide over the ice. It wasn't budging. Frustrated, he slapped a hand against it, and then glanced behind him. Gerda and the others were specks on the horizon, but growing larger by the minute. He needed another way in. Determined, Kai raced along the courtyard walls, looking for a weak spot in the ice. There, in the brightest part of the sunlight, the wall was so thin he could see patches of green and brown on the other side - near her garden.

With a cry of rage, he hefted his spear and slammed the butt of it against the wall.

It cracked, striated lines beginning to form in the ice. Another slam of his spear, and a thick chunk fell at his feet. He continued to jab his spear at it, working furiously until he'd made enough of a hole to see through.

What he saw on the other side chilled him.

There, at the edge of her garden, Charlotte lay collapsed, her hand reaching into the soil as if giving it the last of her powers. Her lovely dress was nearly fully melted, and the white floss of her hair lay in a tangle in the wet brown soil.

She wasn't moving.

"Charlotte," he cried, and attacked the wall with his spear anew. "Charlotte! I'm coming! Hold on for me!"

If she heard him, she didn't stir.

Her lack of response made him redouble his efforts, until he was frantically chipping at the wall with quick, violent strokes. When the hole was almost big enough, he rammed his shoulder against the ice, and it groaned. A second ram and his shoulder throbbed in protest, but he was able to push through, stumbling to the other side.

Then, he got to his feet and raced to her, ripping off his cloak so he could wrap her in it. With infinite tenderness, he lifted her from the ground, cradling her form against him. He wrapped her in the cloak, but her limp hand brushed against his skin.

She...wasn't cold.

The fear he'd been struggling against made his heart stutter in response.

Charlotte, his snow queen, wasn't cold. Her skin was heating, which meant that the powers she depended on had been completely tapped out. She was helpless.

And he suspected she was dying.

With a cry of rage, he clutched her to his chest, rocking her. She was so still, her breathing faint, her cheeks drained of the blueish tint that spoke of her health.

"For weeks, I've dreamed of touching you," he told her in a sorrow-filled voice. His fingers brushed over her skin, her hair, her cheek. "But not like this. Never like this. I will gladly give up any chance to ever touch you again if you'll only open your eyes, Charlotte. Love, open your eyes for me."

But there was no response. Wherever Charlotte was, it was far from him. He bent over her, trying to contain his grief.

"Kai?" Gerda pushed forward through the hole he'd made in the icy fortress wall. "Kai, are you all right?"

He looked up at Gerda, miserable. "She's dying."

"She is?" She stepped forward and then paused, eyeing his expression. "You're upset."

His fingers brushed over Charlotte's lifeless cheek. "She's my mate."

"Your mate?" She gaped. "Her?"

"She is good," he spat at Gerda and her incredulous expression. "You don't know her like I do. She's spent her dying breaths to try and make this land a place that we can all live peacefully in." His heart ached in his breast as if he were the one dying. "She's given everything she had and gotten nothing in return."

"I don't understand, Kai," Gerda said, moving to sit next to him on the ground. She laid her spear in the melting snow. "She kidnapped you and enslaved you."

"That wasn't Charlotte," he said, brushing his fingers along her fine cheekbones and her slack mouth, where her breathing was so, so shallow and faint. "That was the other."

"Explain," Gerda told him, even as others came through the hole in the ice and paused at the sight of him, cradling their enemy so tenderly in his arms.

So he did, holding Charlotte close to him as he told Gerda and the war party about his experiences inside the snow queen's castle. The initial sorcery, the tortures...he glossed over some of those. Then he told them how, a month ago, she'd arrived in his cell, wide-eyed and frightened, and seemingly clueless as to who he was. He told them of her lack of knowledge in simple things - how to feed herself, how to feed him, how to do anything that she'd done with ease just the day before. He told them of her plans to let him go, the day she ran away, and the plants she'd worked so hard to create.

He looked over at those plants now. Small, pale green bushes grew in neat rows in the dirt he'd helped her plow. On a few, he could see pale berries.

She'd succeeded.

"It's not enough to feed us," he told them. "Not yet, but given time, I know she would have. She showed me how to fish through the ice, and creatures to hunt on the far side of the mountain. In time, we could make things work. I know it." He bent his head, pressed his lips to her feverishly warm brow and hated that he couldn't even see a hint of a mark from where he'd pressed his mouth. "She was a prisoner as much as I was."

"Oh, Kai," Gerda said, patting him on the back. "Don't be sad." Her voice was casual, as if she were consoling him over a broken arrow and not the loss of a lover.

"Don't be sad?" he gave her an incredulous look. "She was my mate." He looked down at Charlotte's colorless face, the closed, sunken eyes. "I loved her and would have followed her anywhere."

"Even if she left this land in the grip of eternal winter? Even if you never felt the summer's warmth again?"

"Even so." Warmth was Charlotte's smile when she looked at him, the soft feel of her body next to his in bed. "I would give everything up to remain at her side." He looked at Gerda's discarded spear. "And you came here to kill her."

"Well," Gerda said with an irritated sigh. "I suppose there's no need for that anymore, is there?"

"Oh poop," said an unfamiliar voice. "Is this the part where I say it would have all been possible if it weren't for you meddling kids?"

Chapter Nine

A strange woman strode from the castle itself. She wore an odd pair of baggy yellow pants, a yellow and orange tunic, and a strange shiny yellow hat. She was elderly, her hair white and curly, her face cherubic, and she was stout of figure.

She pushed her way in next to Kai, shoving aside his tribespeople that had gathered around. "All right, all right," she said. "Let me step in and fix things before this little martyr takes everything a bit too far." She leaned in and pinched Charlotte's cheek, cooing. "Who's a little martyr? Who's a little martyr? Yes you are, aren't you?"

"That voice," Kai said slowly, realization dawning. "I recognize it. You were one of the ones she spoke to in the castle. One of her tormentors."

"Now, now, sweet boy." She reached out and pinched Kai's cheek in a grandmotherly fashion. "'Tormentor' is a bit harsh, I think. I prefer to think of myself as a 'motivation specialist'."

"What's going on? Who are you?" Gerda asked, frowning at both Kai and the stranger. "Is this the true snow queen?" She reached for the spear on the ground along-side her.

"Hsst," the old woman said, giving a quick shake of her head. "None of that. You already declared that you weren't going to kill the snow queen, and I don't want you crapping up this happy ever after because you're a little spear-happy." She wiggled her fingers and Gerda's spear melted away into a puff of dust that was carried away on the breeze. "Now. Let me take care of things." She sat next to Kai and took Charlotte's hand. "Wakey-wakey. Naptime's over."

"She's not sleeping," Kai said. This strange woman seemed to have answers and yet...she made no sense. "I cannot rouse her."

"Yes, but you're not a fairy godmother, are you?" She patted Charlotte's hand again. "Come on now, honey. I don't have all day. There are other people to make miserable too, you know."

He opened his mouth to protest...but the bundle in his arms stirred.

"Mmmm?" Charlotte said, her eyelids fluttering. All at once, he felt her grow cold in his arms, the chill seeping through the blankets. Around her, ice crystallized and his breath began to puff in the air. And oh, by all the gods, he'd never been so happy to see that.

"Charlotte," he breathed, overjoyed. He wanted to shout with happiness, but the others were giving them wary looks. He settled for hugging her fur-covered body closer to his. He'd never been so happy to feel the chill of her skin through the furs. "Ah, my mate. Are you all right?"

She blinked up at him as if awakening from a long nap, and then smiled slowly. She was so beautiful. "Kai." Her gaze went to the woman that sat at his side, who'd released Charlotte's hand and was now blowing on her fingers to return the warmth to them. "Muffin?"

"Yes, dearie," the old woman said.

"Why are you dressed like a fireman?"

The one called Muffin threw up her hands. "Because I've been putting out fires all day, honey. Everything always goes to hell in a handbasket at once. Such is the job of a fairy godmother. Everyone decides to make life-changing decisions all at the same time. Terrible for scheduling."

"O-kay," Charlotte said. She rubbed her eyes and seemed to just now realize that there were a lot of people standing around them. As he watched, she shrank a little closer in his arms. "Are they here to kill me?"

"No one's killing anyone," Muffin declared. "Everything has been decided."

Charlotte gave her a wary look, still clinging to Kai's furs. "Then...who won?"

"Doesn't look like anyone won, does it? But I admit, I've never had a draw in a fairy tale before." Muffin tapped her chin thoughtfully. "I'm not quite sure what to do here."

"Please," Charlotte said. "I don't want to leave."

Kai held her tighter against him. He didn't want her to leave, either. She was his, and wherever she went, he wanted to go there, too.

"Well, I can't have a tie on the books," Muffin said. She tilted her round little head. "So either you two duke it out," she pointed at Charlotte and Gerda. "Or I give Charlotte props for creativity and just declare her the winner? I think I'll do that. Then, everyone's happy." She leaned in and gave Charlotte a careful pat. "Job well done."

"Wait, what?" Charlotte struggled to sit up in his arms. "I don't understand." She looked at Kai, then back at the old woman. "You've been discouraging me the entire time! Telling me that I'm doing things all wrong. Telling me that the plants were a bad idea!"

"Well, the plants are a terrible idea. They require so much magic that they're not sustainable. If you move further up the mountain there, above the frost line, then you can live in peace and they can have four seasons again. Winter might be slightly longer, but otherwise, things will be just ducky."

Further up the mountain? Kai glanced up at the forbidding, snow-covered peak. He remembered his day with Charlotte there. She'd seemed happy. And he imagined it would be a small thing to craft a new ice castle amidst the rocky crags if it meant everyone else was well fed and warmth returned to the land.

"I still don't understand why you discouraged me the entire time—"

"It's called 'seeing if you have the stones to do the right thing even when it doesn't benefit you', sweetie. Not everyone gets a fairy tale. You don't think we put this much effort into everyone, do you? I had to make sure you were worthy. And frankly, with the amount of power you were wielding, you could have made this one—" she pointed at Gerda — "into a popsicle and thought nothing of it. Things were a bit lopsided in your favor, so I did my best to try and even things out. Give you a bit more of a challenge."

Charlotte closed her eyes, clearly thinking. "I don't have that much power any more. I destroyed the mirror."

"The mirror wasn't kiddie stuff. I'm glad you didn't play with it. And you don't need that much power. Just stop exhausting yourself on silly bushes and relax and enjoy yourself."

"So...I get to stay?"

Muffin winked. "You get to stay. Have fun with your stud here. I'm off to go try and salvage things on a Cinderella run in Ancient Egypt." She shook her head. "You'd think nobody heard of compromise before. Ah well. Duty calls! Have a nice life, sweetie. And remember what I said - above the frost line. Now, get your strength back and start redecorating." She wiggled her fingers and then disappeared in a puff of pink glitter.

Kai stared at the spot where the woman had been. "Strange sorceress," he murmured.

"Where'd she go?" Gerda demanded. "I still don't have my spear!"

"She left, and I don't know that she'll be back," Kai said. He hoped not. He still couldn't forgive the way she'd tortured Charlotte and made her cry. He squeezed his mate closer in his arms. She was being unusually quiet. He looked down at her beloved face and noticed she'd gone unconscious again. His heart squeezed painfully in his chest at the sight. But her breathing was soft and even, and the faint icy blue had returned to her cheeks. Even now, he felt the cold of her seeping through the furs. "My mate needs to rest," he told the others in a soft voice, so as not to wake her.

Gerda seemed uneasy. "Do you truly think she'll move into the mountains?"

"She will," Kai said. "She's never wanted to hurt anyone. All she wants is to live in peace." And she wouldn't be lonely, because he was going to be there with her, at her side.

Forever.

Charlotte woke up some time later to the feel of a soft fur glove stroking her bare skin. Immediately, her thoughts turned erotic. "Mmm, Kai."

"I'm here," he said softly. The glove moved down her back, glided over a sensitive buttock. "And we're alone. Finally."

Alone...? Oh God. She bolted upright, her mind flashing through vague memories of the day. "I...where are we?"

"You're safe," he told her. "You're in bed. You were exhausted so I carried you in. You've slept most of the day through."

Carried her in? Charlotte rolled onto her back and put a hand to her forehead, trying to think. She'd been so incredibly weak since destroying the mirror, and out of her mind with grief at having to send Kai away. Flashes of vague, dreamlike memory pushed to the forefront: giving the last of her strength to her berry bushes, Muffin's face peering over her own, a fireman's uniform, Kai's own troubled face as he gazed down at her, black streaks on his cheeks...

She pressed a hand to her forehead. "Is it weird that I actually feel pretty good right now?"

"You've had nearly a full day to rest," Kai said in a husky voice, and the soft glove brushed along her skin again. "I imagine that the magic works much like a rain barrel does. Pull too much at once and it will take time to refill, but it eventually will."

That made sense. She opened her eyes, gazed up at the faceted ice ceiling, and then looked into his handsome face. Her hands longed to touch him, but even now, she could feel the heat blasting through his skin that warned her away. "You washed your paint off."

"That was war paint," he said, a dark look on his face.

She froze in place. "Are...are they still outside? Waiting for me to come out to attack?"

"Do you not remember?" The glove caressed her cheek, brushed her hair away from her face. "Your fairy godmother said that if we stay above the frost line, no one shall be affected. They have left, and in a few days, you and I will make our home higher in the mountains."

A sweet ache crept into her throat. "You and I?"

"I'm not leaving you, Charlotte. You're my mate." The glove caressed her cheek, as did his gaze. "You can try to send me away, but I will chip at the ice walls until I break through again. There is nothing you can do that will keep me from your side."

She nodded, swallowing the lump in her throat.

"Why did you send me away before? When you were so sick? I felt as if my heart had been removed from my breast." His soft glove trailed down to her breasts and rested between them. Apparently she was naked.

She didn't care.

She licked her lips, feeling like an ass for hurting him. "Muffin told me that you being here could end up hurting you. I didn't want that." She confessed everything to him - the mirror, Muffin's warnings about the different realities and the way the fairy tale worked out each time. The fairy godmother had sworn her to secrecy before, but since everything was theoretically 'over', she didn't suppose it mattered if she told Kai the truth of everything. "I sent you away because I loved you and wanted to keep you safe," she said finally. "I'm sorry if it hurt you."

"I saw you dying," he said in an agonized voice, and caressed her cheek again. "How could you think it didn't hurt me?"

"I didn't know if I'd get to stay here," she confessed. "And I didn't want you to wake up next to the old snow queen if she came back. I didn't want to do that to you." Her hand went to his covered chest, wishing she could feel his heartbeat. "I couldn't bear the thought of you in her embrace again."

"I would have chanced it if it meant remaining at your side."

She shook her head. No sense in dwelling on something that hadn't come to pass.

"Don't you know you own my heart, Charlotte?" He pressed his gloved hand over her fingers, still resting on his chest. "It's always yours."

Her own heart ached in response. "I love you, Kai. I'm so happy I'm still here with you. You can't imagine how happy."

"Then show me, love," he told her in a husky voice, the look in his dark gaze intense.

She shivered and her hand slid lower on his fur tunic, caressing his cock as she gazed into his eyes.

A voice cleared. "Before you two get busy..."

Charlotte's eyes widened in horror. Oh god, she knew that voice. "Muffin?" Her hand jerked away from Kai's body. A sense of dread swept over her. Was the fairy godmother changing her mind? "I thought—"

"I know, I know," the fairy godmother said, stepping forward. This time she was in a flouncy white dress and straw hat. She looked more like Mary Poppins than a fireman. "But your happy ever after kept bothering me. I mean, if you can't touch, how are we going to have snow babies?"

"Huh?" was her eloquent reply.

"So," the fairy godmother said. "I figured every queen needs her king. When you broke the mirror, it took all your nice little unseen servants with it. And if you're heading up the mountain, you'll be lonely. Real lonely. And nothing heats up a cold winter night quite like *real* company. Now, come here, boy," she said, and grabbed Kai's shoulder and pulled him down to her. Before Charlotte could protest, Muffin gave him a big, smacking kiss on the mouth.

Kai tumbled over backward and fell off the bed.

Muffin giggled, the sound girlish and high. "Two thousand years, and I can still knock them on their asses." She looked over at Charlotte, who was gaping, open-mouthed. "Have fun with your Snow King, sweetie. You won't be seeing me again."

"Snow King?" Charlotte asked, but Muffin was already gone. Glitter rained from the air. She peered over the side of the bed. "Kai? Are you all right?"

He lay on the floor, eyes closed.

Charlotte panicked and leapt off the bed, rushing to his side. "Kai?" She pulled at his tunic, careful not to touch him. His normally warm, tanned face was pale, a hint of blue edging his firm mouth. "Kai? Speak to me."

He opened his eyes and she gave a sigh of relief.

Kai raised a hand into the air and stared at it curiously. His fingers were tipped in ice, and he frowned, then exhaled slowly. His breath came out as a frosty puff.

"Kai?"

He looked over at Charlotte, and then grabbed her and pulled her mouth against his in a fierce, impromptu kiss.

Charlotte stilled, panic flooding through her mind, of burning Kai with her mouth, of the pain and misery that the simple touch could bring...

But he felt...wonderful. She gasped as she realized his mouth was the same temperature as her own.

He laughed between kisses, his hands moving to cup her face as he kissed her over and over again. "Snow King. That old witch is crazy but I think I love her. I'm a Snow King!" He laughed wildly again. "She wanted me to be with my Snow Queen. This is incredible." He kissed her again, and again.

Charlotte was incredulous. "I can't believe it. I—I never thought to ask—" her hands gripped his tunic and then she tore at it, frantic. "Let me touch you. All of you. Please, Kai."

He pulled at the clothing, equally as anxious as her, and they both divested him of the heavy furs within a matter of moments. Charlotte was already naked, and soon enough, he sat before her, his long, heavy black hair tipped with frost at the ends. His chest was as smooth and dusky as ever, but his nipples had a hint of frosty blue to them. She looked further down, unable to help herself. His cock was erect, and oh, it was gorgeous. Her fingers touched the crown of it reverently, still awed that she could actually touch him, and she gave a wild giggle when a bead of pre-cum iced on the head. "This is so incredible, Kai. I just...I can't even...." She shook her head, overcome.

"It's a gift," he said in a low voice, and put his hand behind her neck and pulled her mouth toward him again. "You are mine, and I am yours. We are now a perfect match together. We are blessed."

In this moment, she truly felt blessed indeed. With a happy squeal, she tackled him and rolled on the ground with him. Charlotte felt giddy with joy. He held on to her and they flipped over until she was beneath him and he was above her and his long hair was trailing on her skin.

"And now," Kai told her softly, the look on his face infinitely tender. "I can kiss you as many times as I wish."

"Then kiss me now."

He smiled and bent to kiss her, and his lips moved against her own. And oh, it was sweet and wonderful and delicious. His mouth opened and his tongue touched hers, and she moaned. Just to be able to kiss Kai felt like the sweetest gift in the world, to feel his teeth tug at her lower lip, his tongue caress her own.

They kissed for endless minutes, each movement of his mouth on hers a new and wonderful experience. By the time he lifted his head to give her a chance to catch her breath, she was panting with need and aching between her legs.

"I love that I can caress your soft skin," he told her, his nose nudging her own in a tender gesture that made her feel so, so adored. "I love that I can run my mouth, my tongue, my lips along yours. I love that I can touch your breasts." His hand cupped one, teasing her aching nipple.

"I am yours," she whispered.

"And now that we both have ice at our command, my imagination is full of thoughts on how we can use these powers..." He lifted a hand and ice formed, shaping into...a phallus.

She giggled. "Typical man."

"Your man," he said, leaning in to kiss her again.

"My man," she agreed, putting her arms around his neck. "My man to touch and caress and kiss." She nipped at his jaw, his neck, his shoulder, anywhere she could reach him.

His hand moved down her belly, trailing the ice dildo along her navel, and then gliding it lower. It felt smooth and warm against her skin, like glass. And it excited her when he pressed it lower, the thick length prodding at the curls of her sex.

"This time, it won't be just my fingers entering you," he whispered as he kissed her again. "It will be my fingers, my ice, and my cock. I will have you in every way, my mate."

She trembled at those intense words.

"Open your legs for me, sweet," he murmured, and rubbed the icy creation against her clitoris.

Oh God, that felt like sin itself. Charlotte moaned, her legs falling open so he could pleasure her. There was something naughty - but so right - about him using ice for their mutual pleasure. It was part of who they were and what had brought them together, and it felt natural.

She arched her hips as he continued to rub the ice-cock against her clitoris, the bulb of the head creating delightful friction. Kai kissed her again, and as he did, he pushed it lower. It circled the opening of her core, teasing her, and then he pushed it in, inch by slow inch. She cried out, clinging to him.

"You're so beautiful, my Charlotte," he told her as his lips claimed her again. Slowly, he worked the ice dildo in and out, stroking it. "Beautiful, and mine."

Charlotte clung to him, tangling her hands in his long black hair. His skin felt incredible against her own. Warm, but just right for her. "Kai, I love you so much."

"Charlotte," he murmured, kissing her neck, her throat. "I've changed my mind."

Her heart stuttered slightly to hear that. "Changed your mind?"

"I wanted to make love to you with ice, then fingers, then my flesh. I wanted to drive you wild slowly and savor every moment." The thick length of ice inside her disappeared and for a second, she felt so empty, so bereft, that she whimpered. He leaned in and kissed away the sound. "But now that I have you in my arms, I just want to sink inside you and lose myself."

Oh. "That's what I want, too," she told him softly, and wrapped her legs around his waist. "Please, Kai, I need you so much. I feel as if we've waited forever for this. Let's not wait any longer."

His lips brushed against hers, ever so softly. "From this moment on, you are mine."

With one smooth stroke, his cock filled her, thicker and harder and oh so much better than the ice ever was. Her heart skipped a beat, and a gasp escaped her.

And oh, this was...perfection.

"Kai," she moaned. "Kai. Kai. My Kai. We're joined."

"Together," he agreed, voice rough with emotion. "For now and forever."

She kissed him again, even as he began to move inside her. Each rock of his hips against her own made her want to scream with a mad kind of joy. All thoughts of an orgasm were forgotten in place of sheer and utter happiness. Tears brimmed in her eyes and she clung to him, raising her hips to meet his thrusts. No moment had ever felt so in tune, so intense, so personal.

So perfect.

"My queen," he murmured reverently, his shaft pumping into her over and over again. "My love."

She clung to him, beyond contentment. "Love you, Kai."

But he only gave her a wicked grin and touched the floor beneath her hips. Ice rose under her bottom, making her hips rise up from the ground. It changed the angle of his constant thrusts, and suddenly his next one rubbed against an entirely new place deep inside her...and it made her wild. Her fingernails dug into his back and she whimpered, shocked at how intense it felt. "Oh my God, what was that?"

"That was me showing my insanely powerful wife what her king can bring to the table." He moved again, and she nearly came unglued.

And nearly came, for that matter.

Charlotte sucked in a breath. "Oh dear God. I think that's my G-spot."

"What is that?"

She shook her head and pounded on his shoulder. "Keep doing what you're doing. Don't mind me."

He swiveled his hips in a teasing manner, the smile on his face confident, and brushed against that spot again.

Her legs jerked in response, and she cried out, clinging to him for dear life. Oh God, that felt too intense. Oh God, he needed to do it again and again.

His throaty chuckle was delicious against her throat, but not half as delicious as the next firm stroke that sent her clawing against his shoulders again. His movements sped up, and then all she could do was hold on to him while he screwed her into a wild, screaming, clenching orgasm that took over her body and made her see stars.

And oh, heavens, it was the best thing ever.

Kai came a split second after she did with a grunt that sounded like her name. He stroked into her a few more times, then collapsed on top of her.

She didn't mind the weight of him. Kai's body was bigger than her own, but being able to run her fingers along his shoulders, being able to kiss and caress every inch of skin, being able to rub her feet against his bare legs and feel every inch of his front pressed against her front?

There was no other feeling in the world that could compare. She'd probably touch him for hours on end. Days, maybe.

He propped up on his elbows, beautiful in a spill of black hair over his tanned shoulder. "Should I get up? I'm probably heavy."

"You're not heavy," she told him, dragging him back down. "You're perfect."

Really, everything was perfect.

Epilogue

Everyone said the winter that first year wasn't a terrible one. Oh, sure, it was bitterly cold and the snow stayed knee-high until spring, but the Snow Queen and her King worked hard to ensure that everyone in the valley was happy and well-fed despite the weather. And really, after such a long run of summertime snow, no one minded a few inches more when there was a winter storm.

For the most part, though, life in the valley went back to normal. The Snow King and Queen stayed in the mountains in their ice castle, well above the frost line, and their glittering frozen domain was a wonder tucked high amongst the clouds. The village sent family and friends to visit, heavily laden with furs, and were always welcomed by the frosty little family.

Winters in the valley, though, were a thing of joy. The royal family came down from the keep, the Snow Queen cradling their youngest baby at her breast and the King swinging his toddling son over his shoulders. The children's powers were not quite as strong as their parents, but no one commented on such things. It was impolite, and the little family was so happy, who cared how much magic anyone had?

Once the royal family came down from the mountain, the winter festivals truly began. For weeks on end, children woke up to the sight of new and exciting snow sculptures littering the valley every day. There were mazes to solve, icicle throwing games to play, and delicious snowy treats to devour (though everyone avoided the yellow snow). King Kai was well-loved by his people, and they adored seeing him so happy with his wife and children. And if his wife spoke oddly or wasn't familiar with customs, well that was all right, too. It was clear she loved her husband and children, and equally clear that she used her ice magic only to benefit those around her.

Within a few years, no one remembered the whole 'evil' thing in front of the snow queen's name. They only remembered good Queen Charlotte, who doted on her babies and snuck kisses with her husband.

Clearly the whole 'evil queen' thing was just a fairy tale.

From the Author

Thank you for reading this book! Seriously – thank you. Somewhere out there, a unicorn just farted a rainbow out of sheer happiness. And your hair sure is pretty today! Have you lost weight? No? Well, keep doing what you're doing, because you look fabulous.

Anyhow…

If you are the type that likes to review what you've read, I'd love for you to leave me a review – let me know what you thought. Feedback is super important to people like me that juggle three or more series at once. We love feedback like chocolate loves peanut butter. And the more feedback I get, the more it tells me what I need to work on next. So if you want more Time Travel books, let me know!

About the Author

Jessica Clare is a New York Times and USA Today Bestselling author who writes under three different names. As Jill Myles, she writes a little bit of everything, from sexy, comedic urban fantasy to zombie fairy tales. As Jessica Clare, she writes erotic contemporary romance.

She also has a third pen name (because why stop at two?). As Jessica Sims, she writes fun, sexy shifter paranormals. She lives in Texas with her husband, cats, and too many dust-bunnies. Jill spends her time writing, reading, writing, playing video games, and doing even more writing.

Made in the USA
San Bernardino, CA
13 May 2016